SURVIVOR PLANET TOURNAMENT

JULIET CARDIN

This is a work of fiction. Names, characters, places, and incidents are products of the author's imagination or are used fictitiously and are not to be construed as real. Any resemblance to actual events, locations, organizations, or persons, living or dead, is entirely coincidental.

World Castle Publishing, LLC
Pensacola, Florida

Hardback ISBN: 9798249906580
Paperback ISBN: 9798891265363
eBook ISBN: 9798891265370
Second Edition World Castle Publishing, LLC, March 9, 2026
http://www.worldcastlepublishing.com

Cover: Cover Designs by Karen

CHAPTER 1

He was going to kill me.

If he found me, I was dead meat. Carnage would be my new middle name. Handsome as Kale was to the outside world, I'd seen him for the monster he truly was. He'd end me now. Snap my neck and burn my bones. Dead girls told no tales.

Though my limbs screamed in agony, I pushed onward. At least I wasn't freezing my ass off anymore. My legs slipped and scraped for traction against slick rock while my hands clung to fistfuls of moss. I finally got a toehold and lurched myself up onto the ledge of the steep rock face. I lay still for a moment, sucking in deep breaths of crisp northern air before staggering to my feet.

Exhaustion.

Pure, unconstrained, bone-jarring exhaustion filled every pore of my body from my head down to my well-worn hiking boots. It'd be worth it, though. From here, I was able to see the entire lake and surrounding cottages—a prime vantage point for rat patrol. Aubrey Lake was horseshoe-shaped with a point jutting out brazenly right in the center. It was there my cottage sat, sticking out like a sore thumb. Stupidly, I'd thought coming here would be safe. But no, he'd arrived after noon, just when I'd begun to relax. He'd been here only once before, at the end of last summer, over eight months ago. It was a six-hour drive just to reach town, then zigzagging roads, corkscrew turns, and a practically hidden turn-off to the lake. Surely he wouldn't remember the route?

He'd found me anyway.

After all, Tenacity was his middle name.

I took in the sight of the thick forest below, just beginning to turn green with new spring leaves. All was silent, even the birds, as if the entire forest was holding its breath and watching me. As comforting as the expanse of nature felt, I knew it was a lie. Danger lurked everywhere. None so much as my bent-on-killing-me boyfriend. I needed time to sit and think, time to regroup and plan, if my next move was not to be my last. And this place, though high and away, was not it. Far below at the water's edge, my bright yellow canoe rested. A glaring beacon giving my location away. I comforted myself with the knowledge that, unless he stole one, it was the only boat available. To get to me, he'd have to hike down the road and up the trail to reach this location. If I wanted the advantage of a lead, I needed to move. Now.

I gave the area another careful look and moved on. The forest behind me stretched out for miles; you could get lost in it for days, which was exactly what I intended to do. I had a pretty good sense of direction, so when enough time passed that Kale grew bored and hopefully went home, I'd emerge. Until then, I'd live off the land. How difficult could it be?

There was a cave way in the back forty I'd hiked to on many occasions with my aunt and uncle—God rest their souls. Uncle Mick had dragged me from one end of the eternal forest to the other since they'd bought this place seventeen years ago. I'd been three at the time and rambunctious as hell. The perfect hiking partner for my childless guardians. How I wished Mick were here now. He'd punch Kale in his perfectly rugged face and then kick his gorgeous ass all the way back to Havelton—our hometown. What a fool I'd been not to see the ugliness beneath Kale's striking shell. At least, not till it was too late.

A drop of sweat ran down my back, and I could feel moisture gathering in my armpits. A few days out here with no amenities, and Kale would probably run in the opposite direction if he did find me. I stopped for a moment when the trail began to wane. I was at the halfway point. It got a bit dicey from here. The logical part of my brain always questioned my direction, while my gut usually assured me to trust my instincts. I'd never gotten lost yet. And yeah, I'd come up here alone before. Last summer, in fact. Right before I happened to meet 'Mr. Wonderful'. Sucker that I'd been, I couldn't wait to rush him up here and show him the glorious north. I'd been all about sharing back then. Full of happily ever afters, rainbows, kittens, and riding off into sunsets. What a dolt. Being orphaned once more, just a couple of months before we met, I'd jumped into a relationship with an older man with both feet.

Kale was supposed to save me. Supposed to be my knight in shining armor. My hero. And he had been. For six glorious months, he'd been the most incredible catch on Earth.

Then everything went to shit.

All of a sudden, his personality seemed to punch into overdrive. He questioned everything I did and everywhere I went. I had no family, and he didn't want me to have any friends either. Not that I had many. I'm kind of a recluse by nature. We lived together in his apartment by that time. A small two-bedroom in a high-rise—the seventh floor to be exact. I got to see how far up we were quite intimately when he grabbed my hair and bent me backward over the railing. Then there was the time he punched a hole through the wall right beside my head.

Good times.

I suppose I should have taken these little hints to be signs of bigger things to come, but no. Fool that I'd been, I'd made excuses. He'd had a hard day at work. He was tired. He was sick. He was under pressure. I wasn't doing enough to help out financially. I didn't clean the apartment well enough. I wasn't attentive enough. Things will be better tomorrow…You know, the regular bullshit we tell ourselves to sleep at night.

Last week was the last straw…

I heard the snap of a branch.

"Mandy?" His voice washed over me like a cold shower, and goose bumps spread across my arms despite the sweat covering my skin.

Damn it to hell, would I never escape?

Slowly, I turned around. His face blurred for a moment, and instead of seeing Kale—brutal and beautiful—I saw two men in white jumpsuits. The one in the front held up his hands and moved forward on cautious feet as if I were a woodland creature he was trying not to spook.

"Everything's all right, Amanda. You're safe now. Just come back with Danny and me, and you'll see."

"Danny?" My eyes flashed to the other man,

who stared back at me with a bit of a smirk.

"Yes, you remember Danny, don't you? And me? Come on now, sweetheart, we're friends, remember?"

My mind jolted, and flashes of my past began to return, running through my head like a bad movie. "Jack?" Yes, that was his name. I'm pretty sure it was.

"Yes, it's Jack. See, you do remember." Closer he came, stalking me until he was only a few feet away. Despite our proximity, he didn't reach out to touch me.

Reality pecked away at me until the blurry line between fact and fiction began to clear. I looked down at my feet and noticed I was wearing white running shoes. What the hell? Where were my boots? The trees around me were suddenly lush and green, and the air was warm—almost too warm. It was spring, wasn't it? Why was everything suddenly different? I held up my arms in front of me. Bare. I should be cold, but I wasn't. My clothes, not jeans and a long-sleeved cotton shirt and a jacket, but a plain white gown reaching just above my knees.

"Jack?" He took my hand when I reached out. I clung to him shamelessly. "What's happening to me?"

Laughter sounded. Danny was shaking his head, and I heard him mutter the word, 'Loon'.

Jack turned and hissed something at him while putting a comforting arm around my shoulder. He pivoted and began to lead me down the pathway in the direction I'd just come. I froze. "No! Kale, he's coming. He'll get me."

More laughter from Danny. "Not likely, doll," he said. I didn't like his voice. It was harsh like Kale's.

"Mandy, no one's gonna get you," Jack assured me. "Kale is in your mind, remember? He's not real. We talked about this last week."

Not real? What'd he mean? Of course, Kale was real. I knew everything about him. How his hair felt when I ran my fingers through it. How he smelled like Old Spice and something rugged. I knew how his hands felt on my body when he made love to me. I knew how the sound of his voice, when raised in anger, made me cringe and shake with fear. The sound of his taunting laughter was what made me run away. Yes, I remember now. I'd heard it all around me. He'd been coming to get me, and he would hurt me again. He always hurt me. And nobody believed me. No one helped me. So I had to run, had to save myself…

The pieces came to me like a broken puzzle, trying to put itself back together. I'd been outside in the yard with the others. My mind had been clear and calm, so they'd left me alone to wander. At the edge of the forest, I'd seen the hole in the fence. The others sat on benches or played with dolls. One of them was arguing with an attendant—Daisy Mellville—that was her name. She was a troublemaker, and I didn't like her. Peering over my shoulder, I saw more attendants in the yard rush up and try to calm her. It was then that Kale's voice and cruel laughter came to me. Loud and mean. Even though I covered my ears with my hands, I could still hear it. Ignore it. I'd tried. Really, I did. Even hummed a little and began reciting the six wives of Henry the Eighth, but nothing worked.

The hole in the fence yawned wide like a big cavern, beckoning me, lulling me with safety…and escape. What choice did I have but to take it? It was either run or wait for Kale to come and get me. So I did what I had to do.

I ran.

CHAPTER 2

Jack continued to guide me down the pathway. After a few minutes, he released me and took up the lead. I plodded along obediently. Danny walked behind us, and self-consciously, I felt his eyes upon me. My gaze took in the beautiful August day. Birds were singing, flowers were blooming, insects buzzed, and critters crept. Why I'd thought it was spring was another item to add to my already long list of mysteries.

The droop of Jack's shoulders told me I'd led them on a merry chase. How much of it had been real, I wasn't sure. The canoe part was sketchy. Sure, I could paddle one well enough, so it could have happened. I'm sure I'd climbed the big rock face as well. My aching limbs gave testament to that little stunt. The cottage at the point had once belonged to my aunt and uncle. Now it was held in trust for me, as was their entire estate, me being their only heir. They were dead and had been for much longer than a year. More like four. I'd been sixteen at the time. And since that time, when I was discovered rocking back and forth amongst the blood and guts, I'd been the youngest resident ensconced in the Lindove Asylum.

To this day, I couldn't tell you what happened. My only memory of the Event is that Uncle Mick and Aunt Erin, and I had been sitting around the fireplace after eating dinner. All at once, things had started to rattle like an earthquake, and then a bright white light blazed in through every window. After that, nothing. No memories. No anything. Not until I snapped out of my trance three days later and learned I was no longer at the cottage. I'd been bundled up and taken to the asylum.

They'd been kind to me at Lindove. They'd filled me in on the Event, gently and with a great deal of sympathy. Told me that someone must have killed my guardians and decided, for some unknown reason, to let me live. No one had been caught and punished for the crime. To this day, the whole thing remains a mystery.

For the most part, I liked Lindove. It was situated in the small northern town of Graneden, not far from the cottage I'd loved so much. I felt safe there. Well, most of the time, that is. It was only when I had an Episode—became all weird and stuff—and people would look at me as if I was crazy, that I didn't like it. Not that it happened often, but when it did…

We reached the rock face, and Jack helped me

climb back down. Behind me, I could hear Danny doing a lot of swearing. He'd said "pain in the ass" several times, and I knew he was talking about me. At the bottom of the hill rested the canoe, gently rocking against the shore in the lapping waves. So, I had taken it then. The poor guys had had to take the long way round to get me. No wonder Danny was annoyed. Jack maneuvered the canoe so he could sit in the back. Danny climbed in the front, and I sat in the middle. I didn't get to paddle. Once across the lake, we all got out, and the men pulled the boat up onto the shore and tipped it over. I was pretty impressed I'd managed that feat all on my own. I guess fear was a pretty big motivator.

Since the Event, the huge, faceless man of my nightmares had haunted me mercilessly. First, only when I slept, but then, over the past eight months, he'd begun to appear when I was awake. Gradually, his face became clearer, until one day I could see him as well as I saw anyone else. The only problem was that no one else ever saw him. He was really careful, see, only showing up in empty corridors or empty rooms, and always when I was alone. It didn't help that my mind got confused a lot. I'd thought naming him would be a good idea, so he became Kale. Kale began visiting me so often that I'd begun to think of him as my boyfriend.

Call it wishful thinking, coping, or just plain crazy, but I invented an entirely new reality in which Kale and I had fallen madly in love and moved in together. Of course, he'd been insanely jealous over anyone else in my life—he loved me that much. In fact, he loved me so much that he became obsessed with me. I'd never had a boyfriend, but I'd heard some of the older women in here talk about it. One of them had been so in love she'd actually tried to kill her boyfriend. None of them had had what you'd describe as a healthy relationship—at least, according to the doctors. Sometimes this fantasy life I'd created got confused with my real life. I got all mixed up with what was real and what was not. In the middle of the night, I'd wake up in a cold sweat, sure that Kale was just outside my door. I can't exactly remember when I started to be afraid of him. My fantasy had gotten out of control over the months, and the more I imagined Kale loving me, the more I figured he'd become obsessed, and then violent. I hadn't meant for things to become like this between us. It was just that, listening to the other patients, it seemed to me that all relationships turned bad eventually.

Jack and Danny had parked the white van with the little dove emblem out front of the cottage. I kept my eyes focused on the dove while I walked, not daring to look at the cottage. Seeing it brought back painful memories, and I wondered why I'd dared to come here. I got the creeps just being close to it.

"Should be home just in time for dinner," Jack said. He smiled kindly at me and even winked as he pulled open the sliding door and ushered me inside. Danny jumped into the passenger seat in the front, and after Jack slid the door shut, he climbed behind the wheel of the van. From the backseat, through the windshield, I could see the cottage clear as day. I kept my eyes directed up over the roof at the sky. It'd begun to grow dim out since it was getting on in the year. No more bright sunshine till nine o'clock. Now it was practically full dark by eight. Dinner was always at six o'clock sharp, so I knew it was getting late. Jack put the van into reverse and began to back up to curve around the driveway so he could straighten out the van and drive out. All of a sudden, he slammed on the brakes.

"Damn!" he swore, which was out of character for him.

"What's wrong now?" Danny demanded. I knew he didn't like to miss meals, always being cranky before lunch and dinner. The small paunch of a stomach he sported had grown a good size over the years.

"The door's wide open," Jack said, gesturing

towards the cottage. "You guys sit tight, and I'll check it out." He didn't wait for a reply before he put the van into park and jumped out. Danny just snorted in agitation, sending me a glare that told me how annoyed he was. As soon as Jack was out of hearing range, Danny lit into me.

"How the fuck did you get out here anyway? Hitch a ride, you little tramp? I bet some old guy diddled you the whole way."

Used to his attacks, I ignored him. Despite not wanting to look, I watched as Jack entered the cottage and disappeared from sight. For some reason, seeing him step into the void made me extremely worried. The laughter began again, Kale's cruel voice drumming inside my head. Even when I put my hands up to cover my ears, it still continued on.

"Shut up! Shut up!" I began to holler, rocking back and forth in my seat.

Danny looked at me like I was an even bigger freak than I was. "What the fuck? You shut up. Shut your damn mouth!" His loud yelling joined in with Kale's until I couldn't differentiate between them. I shut my eyes tight.

Suddenly, he pounded his fist against the dashboard, making my eyes bulge open in fear. Everything stopped. The voices, the yelling—

everything but the fear. Something was wrong. Very wrong.

Jack hadn't come back out. Why he was taking so long was anyone's guess. Danny swore in frustration and climbed out of the van. He slid open the side door and told me to get out. With me in the lead—not by choice—we began walking towards the open door of the cottage. My heart started racing, and my breath became heavy in my chest. Every step I took was like walking towards the executioner's block. I hadn't crossed the threshold since the Event, and even though Danny was with me and Jack was inside, I didn't want to do it now. When I reached the door, I hesitated.

"Inside," Danny growled.

My hand shook as I reached for the screen door. It was the heavy wooden door that had been left open. I stared at it once the screen was wide enough to step past. Scorch marks were scarred across the deep red paint as though left by the fiery hand of a dragon. When my feet refused to move, Danny gave me a not-so-gentle shove from behind. I practically fell into the room beyond.

"Jack?" Danny yelled over my head. He walked around me and went into the living room, where there was a fireplace and a big picture window that faced out towards the lake. To my right was the galley kitchen. Just beyond that was a long hallway with doors leading to a bathroom and bedroom on the right, and another two bedrooms on the left. The entire cottage felt completely still, yet not quite empty. My eyes darted around, searching the corners in the dim light, expecting something terrible to spring forth.

"Where are you, Jack?" Danny demanded. He began stalking down the hallway and systematically opened each of the closed doors. At the last door, he hesitated. He turned to look at me from where I'd wandered another few steps and could now see down the hall. I wanted to shout at him not to open the door. There was no reason why that I could logically explain, but whatever was behind it, I felt should stay hidden. Danny smirked at me, and his hand reached for the knob.

That's when everything began to shake. Just like I remembered from four years ago—it's how the nightmare had begun. As the door swung open, I saw Danny raise a hand to his eyes as a blinding white light shot out. He turned away and took one step before he gripped the wall as though something had a hold of him. This time, when his eyes met mine, they were full of fear.

"Jack?" I yelled. Danny was pulled back into the room, slowly, his nails grabbing at the wall, fingernails leaving scratches. Once he disappeared from view, the door slammed shut. "Jack, Danny needs help!" The floorboards continued to rumble and shake, and when I backed up towards the door, my legs were unsteady. I moved in slow motion, like the way I sometimes did in dreams when I was trying to get away.

Blinding light suddenly lit up every window, and I had to sink to the floor and cover my eyes to escape the glare. I spun round and crawled forward, but the scorched wooden door slammed shut, making me turn back toward the living room. I got in front of the fireplace and faced the other door—the one leading to the front deck—before everything stopped and became still. The light was gone, and slowly I got to my feet. It was then that I became aware I was no longer alone.

I turned in resignation, ignoring the screaming voice in my head that urged me to flee, and faced my tormentor. The man who'd hounded me endlessly, first as a nightmare, then as my lover, then as my enemy, since I was sixteen years old.

"Kale?"

He stood tall and unmoving, his face a mask of cold determination. "Ayres, actually," he said.

"For real?"

His hand reached out, and unwillingly, I moved

forward to take it in mine.

He smiled. “For real.”

CHAPTER 3

Just like all those years ago, I awoke with a head full of cotton and a dry mouth. This time, however, the now familiar pristine white walls of Lindove did not surround me. Instead, everything was cold metal. And bars.

I became aware I was curled up on the floor in a thick, rough blanket that scratched at my skin. The floor was clean and bare and looked to be made of concrete. Was I in jail? It would explain the barred window at the top of the imposing steel door of the cell.

There'd been an earthquake, I remembered that, and the bright light. Then…there'd been Kale, yet he'd said his name was Ayres. I'd taken his hand. After that, everything was a blank. A terrible thought entered my mind. Had Jack and Danny been found dead, just like Uncle Mick and Aunt Erin had?

Shit!

Maybe they thought I was a killer. I mean, to have the same crime committed in the same place, leaving only me alive, was pretty convenient. It definitely smacked of guilt. But I hadn't killed anyone.

It was a mistake. I got up on shaky knees and used the wall for leverage as I climbed to my feet. That's when I noticed I was naked. The blanket had pooled around my feet. I reached down and snatched it up, pulling it around my shoulders, and crept toward the door. I peered through the bars, and from what I could see, it appeared I was in some sort of cellblock. A prison, no doubt. They'd locked me up in a place nowhere near as nice as Lindove this time.

From my vantage point, it was impossible to see too far. There was a cell directly across from mine, and I noticed the bob of a head just below the bars. I waited until the head came up again and called out, "Hey. Hello?"

A small pale face framed by a riot of dark curls came into view. "Hello?" a young female's voice answered.

"My name's Mandy. What is this place?"

"I…I dunno. Been here for a few…days…I think." She took a moment to get out her words. Maybe her throat was as dry as mine?

"Did you do something? Something bad?" Must be a prison for women.

"No. Nothing. There was…bright light. A man…"

What? Sounded like the same shit I'd seen.

"What's your name?" Dammit, I needed water.

"Lissa."

"Lissa?" Sounded like a lisp.

"Yeah," she said. "Oh, no! Someone's…coming." She ducked out of sight. When I heard the steady tread of boots in the hall, I did the same, moving as far back as my cell would allow. I wrapped up tightly in the blanket and sat down, trying to conceal my nakedness as my cell door began to rattle. A moment later, it swung open. A very large man stood in the doorway.

Perhaps it was the poor lighting, or my fanciful, if somewhat crazy imagination, but it appeared half of the man's head was made of metal. I squinted my eyes and blinked several times before I confirmed my suspicion. Yep, definitely metal.

"Rise," he said, his voice gruff and as cold as my ass had been on the floor. Despite what was assuredly a wild Episode I was having, I didn't want to take any chances, so I rose to my feet.

"Come," he said, gesturing me forward.

Taking a big gulp, I did as instructed. He reached out suddenly and snatched my blanket away, tossing it behind him.

"Hey!" I made a move to retrieve it, but froze when he raised a hand to strike me. He wore a long gray lab coat over his clothing, which appeared to be a one-piece black jumpsuit. Lowering his hand, he reached into his pocket and removed a strange handheld instrument. I stood stiffly with embarrassment as he waved the device over my midsection and then lower toward my womanly parts. The object hummed, and little lights flashed on and off. He grunted with satisfaction before he put the device away.

Then he left, just like that. He only paused to pull the door shut and lock it behind him. Snatching up the blanket, I peeked through the bars and saw that he'd gone into Lissa's room. He hadn't bothered to shut her door after he entered, either. I suppose with his great bulk, the odds of getting past him were slim to none. The cyborg dude must have yanked off her blanket as well, cause I heard her howl in protest. The word "pervert" was yelled more than once. Apparently, she wasn't as smart as me, cause I heard a loud smack and then a cry—it hadn't come from him.

Quick as he'd been in my cell, he wasn't much longer in hers. When he turned to leave, I ducked down until I heard the click of his boots head off down the hallway. I could hear choking sobs, and I knew Lissa was upset. I'd been a little disturbed by the encounter myself. Instead of calling out to her, I curled up against the back wall and wondered what was going on. Just where in the hell was I? What had happened in the cottage? And where were Jack and Danny? Dead or alive?

My mind jumped from one scenario to another, hashing out this concept or that one over and over—there was nothing else to occupy me. The next thing I knew, the bottom slat of my door slid open, and a tray was shoved inside. Dinner, I guessed. I stretched out and grabbed it, dragging it back to the wall where I could get a look at it. The food at Lindove had been decent. Much more so than this shit. Whatever it was. A single bowl held what appeared to be watery porridge, or maybe it was stew, with chunks of green stuff in it. The awful sight aside, the smell was enough to put me off. There was a mug with plain water in it. I drank it down much too fast and then regretted not rationing it. God only knew when I'd get more. I poked my finger in the mush and then put it in my mouth. Damn, I was hungry. Couldn't remember the last time I ate. The taste was bland but not terrible. They hadn't bothered to give me a spoon. Using my fingers, I scooped up the mush, eating every last bite, then settled back against the wall to see if it'd stay down. When my gut remained calm, I got to my feet and moved to peer out the door.

All was silent across the hall. Lissa was probably gagging down her bowl of crap as well. She'd been here a few days, so she was probably used to the hospitality by now. About an hour or so later—I guessed—the single dim light on the ceiling in my cell went out. Judging by the dark corridor, I presumed it was lights out and time to sleep. Too bad I wasn't tired. My mind was far too wired.

Once more, I pondered my dilemma until sleep finally overtook me. When I awoke, the light over my head was back on again. My bowels were crampy, and I really needed to use the bathroom.

"Lissa, are you awake?" Hopefully, she'd know how things worked in this joint. When I saw her head pop up through the bars, I sighed in relief. "I gotta go to the bathroom, what should I do?"

"Someone'll come soon to take you down," she told me.

Damn, I hope so.

Sure enough, I heard the heavy clip-clop of boots coming down the hall. The cyborg dude opened the door, and I was actually relieved to see him. When he ushered me out the door, I didn't hesitate to obey. We walked down the long cellblock, and I counted the heavy doors as I passed. Six. There were more in the other direction, but I wasn't sure how many. Placing his thumb on a scanner, my guide opened a doorway and led me inside. It was a large room with a row of toilets in it—metal, of course—and a row of metal sinks on the other side. In the back area, it appeared to be open showers.

"Knock on this door when you are finished." He left and shut the door behind him.

Since I was the only one in the room at the moment, I had a semblance of privacy. If I hadn't needed to pee so badly, the cold metal toilets would have forced that issue soon enough. I glanced around as I did my business and then washed my hands. There were no mirrors, so I had no idea how I looked. My blanket was pooled on the floor, and I covered myself up before I knocked on the door to be let out. I was surprised when the cyborg led me, not back to my cell, but down a different hall. The scowl he sported made me hesitate to ask.

Hall after hall we traipsed down, and then we got into an elevator and shot up a couple of floors. When we headed down another long corridor—this one with windows along the right side—I gaped and had to stop.

Holy crap, that's outer space outside!

The cyborg—he might actually be a cyborg—noticed I wasn't trailing obediently behind and turned to snap at me. "Come!"

"But...but..." I gestured grandly at the view.

He smirked. "If you look hard, you may spot

Earth." Then he had the audacity to wink at me.

I turned to the window and stared, as instructed, to search for Earth. Generously, my guide even helped to point it out. Yep. There it was. Good ole Earth. Just as it appeared in all those space shots I'd seen on television.

If I hadn't known before, I now knew beyond a shadow of a doubt—I was certifiably nuts.

CHAPTER 4

"Where are you taking me?" He'd had to take my arm to encourage compliance.

"You will see."

Not much for words, this one. His scowl was back, but I wouldn't let it discourage me from nagging. Not when I was clearly having an Episode. Come to think of it, I'd never actually realized I was having an Episode mid-Episode before. Maybe I was improving?

Just when I was about to start with more questions, the cyborg thumb-printed a door, and when the light went from red to green, he opened it. Ushering me inside, we entered a vast room, circular in shape. The view from the many large windows was stunning—dark space all around with shiny little stars sparkling everywhere. A table curved around half the wall, and seven men were seated. All of them wore the one-piece black jumpsuits from what I could see, except that the shoulders and chest area were colored either green or red. Perhaps I was having an Episode on board the Enterprise? I scrutinized the faces staring back at me, expecting to see television stars, but I didn't recognize any of them—except for one—Ayres. I wasn't surprised. He seemed to star in all my Episodes. Catching my gaze, he inclined his head in a way of greeting. Playing it cool, I copied his gesture.

Cyborg led me to the center of the floor. "Earthling one-five-six. Under the protection of… Ayres." Was it just me, or did he sneer a little?

"Very good. Thank you, Gol. You may leave us," said the man with the red shoulders sitting directly in the middle of the others.

Gol the cyborg nodded, turned, and briskly strode from the room, leaving me alone and naked, except for the blanket. The man who'd addressed Gol scrutinized me, and I squirmed under his gaze. He must be the leader, I surmised.

"This is your entry?" he said to Ayres.

"Yes, Sir Baynar," Ayres said.

He nodded his head after staring at me for a moment. "She is small like the others. I agree to it." He turned to the men on the panel. "What say you?"

"Aye," they all agreed in unison.

"Pathetic little things," Baynar said.

Ayres shrugged his shoulders. "She complies with the regulations."

What the hell are they talking about? And for that matter, why were they discussing me like I wasn't even in the room? God, this felt too damn real. My other Episodes were life-like but kind of fuzzy, as though a dream. This didn't feel like that.

"Drop your blanket," Baynar said to me, so much for being ignored.

"Pardon?"

His eyes flashed, and the hand he rested on the table clenched into a fist. "Can she not hear?"

"She is perfect, I assure you," Ayres said, turning a hard glare on me.

Episode or not, I wasn't about to show these guys my goods.

Before I could say a word, Ayres got to his feet and was beside me. He took hold of my blanket and wrenched it from my body. I tried to snatch it back, but his hands gripped it tight.

"What the fuck?" I snapped, vainly trying to cover my boobs and my bush. Unfortunately, my long dark hair was still in a heavy braid down my back, so I couldn't use it for a shield.

"Stand straight and don't move—if you want to live," Ayres threatened. His voice had been low, just for my ears, but deadly serious. The look in his eyes warned me.

Burying my shame, I dropped my hands to my sides and froze. My chin rose determinedly, but I refused to make eye contact with anyone.

It seemed an eternity before Baynar had his fill. "She is acceptable." The other men voiced their agreements while Ayres covered me back up. "You may return her to her cell."

"Thank you, sir," Ayres said.

As he began to lead me from the room, the leader called to him, and Ayres stopped. "I trust you will fill her in on everything?"

"Yes, sir."

"The tournament will begin tomorrow morning. Be in position…and…good luck to you."

Ayres nodded and led me from the room.

I spun on him as soon as the door shut behind us. "What the hell is going on?"

"Keep your voice down," he snapped. He didn't speak to me again until we got inside my cell. The door shut, and with him inside, the room suddenly seemed much smaller. I'd been biting my tongue and biding my time, but now, looking at the giant before me, I suddenly grew wary.

What if this was real?

"Sit if you prefer," Ayres said. "You will listen to what I have to say, and then you must rest."

I sat.

As he gathered his thoughts, I studied him.

He was much more lifelike than the other times I'd seen him. Imagined him. I corrected myself. Yet, if he were only a figment of my imagination, then how did I know him so well? Ever since I'd lost my aunt and uncle, he'd been there. Of course, I'd fabricated the way we'd met, dated, and fallen in love. Easily, I'd slipped into another life, one separate from life at Lindove. Over time, it'd become easier to do. That Kale—Ayres—would eventually turn into a violent, obsessive boyfriend had been inevitable. Perhaps, in a way, my mind was healing from its turmoil, and the only way to get back to reality was to force Ayres away—make him so unlikable I'd have to let him go? My last Episode had me fleeing him in terror. Maybe I was not fleeing Ayres per se, but attempting to escape a return to reality?

But I knew how his lips felt on my body—everywhere. I knew how the rippling muscles on his bare chest felt against my hands. Knew how warm our bellies felt pressed together, and how I rejoiced when he entered me.

How could I if he wasn't real?

Looking at him now, I felt a warm blush on my cheeks, just thinking of him between my thighs…

"The game begins tomorrow. It's more of a tournament, actually," he said, his deep voice and serious face snapped my mind out of the gutter.

"There will be five couples competing. Each of the males is from my world. The females are from various locations on Earth."

Though I longed to scoff or snort—anything to make him realize how ridiculous this all sounded—I kept silent.

"On board this ship are all the competitors. We will be sent down to Planet Taleon and must be in position by the appointed hour. From there, each team must survive for a total of zexeudn—or, one earth week. We must battle the elements, the wildlife, the Varlings—inhabitants—and each other."

"I have to battle you?"

"No. The teams may engage each other in order to increase their chances for survival."

"Engage in what way?"

"The easiest way to destroy the other team is to maim or kill the female. I must keep you alive in order to win."

I nodded. "And if I die?"

"Then I cannot win."

"What do you get if you win?" I asked.

He actually appeared embarrassed at my question. "I will be granted a boon. It is why I entered the game."

"To be granted a boon?" Dare I ask what that would be?

"Yes," he said.

"I see." Not really, but I could humor him. "What if more than one team wins?"

"The game is not only one of survival, but also a race to the finish. The first team to the Safe Zone will win."

"And what happens to the others?" Do I really want to know?

"They do not leave Taleon. Ever."

Okay then. "Are there judges?"

"The judges are aboard the ship. We will be monitored, and my entire world will be watching."

No pressure there.

"The game is carried out only once an eundn—a year on Earth. I was fortunate to be worthy. In comparison, it is similar in popularity to Earth's Olympics."

"Maybe in the early days when people were fed to the lions," I said. "Our modern games don't entail people battling for their lives."

He shrugged. "It's how things are done on my world."

His world. Was I completely bananas? How had my Episodes gotten so far out of control? I closed my eyes and opened them several times, willing Ayres to disappear, for the cell to disappear, and in its place would be my nice little room at Lindove. But every time I opened my eyes, there was Ayres, watching me with that cold, calculated look on his face.

"Accept your fate," he told me.

Indeed, I had. I'd finally gone completely over the edge of sanity.

CHAPTER 5

"What is the name of your world?" If I had completely flipped into another reality, I may as well accept it. At Lindove, I probably lay comatose in my bed, blankly staring up at my ceiling while the nurses and doctors shook their heads in defeat. That thought was more comforting than worrying I might be acting this scenario out, just as I had the last one. As my Episodes escalated over the past few months, I'd begun to live them, not only in my mind, but with my body as well. I never knew where I was gonna end up when I finally did come out of one. I suppose having vivid visions was better than wandering the darkness of my own mind alone.

"Calixtus."

"And this planet where the game is played—Taleon, you said—don't they mind you guys using their world for extracurricular activities?"

He smirked. "Varlings do not object. They have neither the ability nor the understanding to dispute what a superior race does on their planet. They enjoy the hunt—it is all they care about."

What arrogance. "Are they animals then?"

He seemed to ponder my question before he answered. "I would best describe them as similar to early Earthlings—how your race was before my race became involved."

"So you mean like Cavemen? And what do you mean by before your race became involved?"

"Calixtus was highly advanced long before your planet got out of the Stone Age. Once it became habitable for us, we used it for our early tournaments."

"Are you saying you first played the game on Earth? And that the losers left behind are the ancestors of modern-day man?" This was some trip I was having. Vaguely, I recalled some of the alien conspiracy shows I'd seen on TV. There were theories of an alien race being seen as gods, and suggestions that some of them may have bred with early man in experiments. One of them went so far as to say that criminal or outcast aliens were forced to breed with early Earthlings to create a more intelligent race to be used as slaves. I had to be more careful about what shows I watched in the future lest they become part of an Episode.

"I'm not entirely certain how Earthlings came to be what they are today—history was not my best subject. Over time, a problem emerged. Earth became overpopulated and over-industrialized, making it unsatisfactory for our purposes.

Well, lucky us. "But not so much that you're above nabbing helpless females now and again to use in your games?" So what if I was being sarcastic?

He shrugged and actually smiled, becoming more handsome in that instant. "Earth provides a wide range of entertainment."

Provides. Present tense.

"Helpless females are not the only things we extract," he informed me.

I raised an eyebrow. Did I really want to hear this stuff?

"Men of Earth have proven quite formidable in other tournaments held on Calixtus, as does your wildlife."

A vision of gladiators fighting lions and each other popped into my head. What the hell went on on Calixtus? Were they no better than the blood thirsty Romans from days of old?

"Don't scowl at me like that," Ayres said. "If it weren't for my race, yours would still be living in caves trying to figure out how to make fire."

"I suppose we owe Stonehenge and the Pyramids to you as well?"

He smiled wickedly again. Damn his handsome ass!

My stomach grumbled suddenly, reminding me I hadn't eaten today—at least not in this reality. They were probably feeding me through tubes and IVs in the real world. Ayres eyed my belly, which made me recall how Gol had waved that strange device over my gut and lower. I was pretty sure he'd done the same thing to Lissa. "That guy, Gol. He had this hand-held thingy, and he waved it around my belly," I said.

"Yes."

"Well?"

"Well, what?" Ayres replied.

How exasperating. "What was he doing?" I swear he was being obtuse on purpose.

"Making sure you were unspoiled," Ayres said, as though it were obvious.

"Spoiled in what way? Like my parents gave me everything, or in a rotten banana kind of way?"

"That you are untouched by a man—a virgin," he said the word as though it amused him.

My face grew warm, and I knew I was blushing. Of course, I was a virgin—unless my erotic fantasies starring the man before me had actually occurred. How strange it was to know how his hands felt on my body. Despite being made up exploits in my mind, it had felt real to me. Ayres moved closer, which made me back up until I felt my ass hit the wall behind me.

"What're you doing?" I squawked, seeing a strangely intent look in his eye.

"You will only be touched by my hand. No other man will know you," he informed me in a deep, husky voice.

A tremor raced through me.

"Are…all the women taken virgins?" I asked.

"For now," he assured me.

The sheer size and strength of him frightened me, but along with fear, I began to feel something else. A heat between my thighs and a tingling in my breasts made me duck my head in embarrassment. Why did I feel this way? In my Episodes, Ayres had taken me many times, in many different ways. We'd been lovers before, and even after he'd turned into a monster. Some of the wild, frantic, near-violent sessions we'd engaged in, when he'd turned my rebelling body into a willing, throbbing mass of need, were some of the best Episode sex I'd ever had. Too bad it hadn't been real. Perhaps if it had been real, I wouldn't be here right now. I wouldn't fit the bill if I were 'spoiled'.

Damn my virgin ass!

Breathing deep, I regained control of my emotions; both fear and horniness. This wasn't real, I reminded myself. So what if Ayres wanted to have me? He'd had me before. Even if this felt incredibly authentic, it wasn't. The sex would be amazing. Not some hazy, dream-like coupling. Not this time.

I looked him directly in the eye and let my blanket slip a little so it barely covered the tops of my breasts. My invitation didn't escape him. He smiled and reached out a hand to gently brush atop my cleavage, making me shiver with desire.

"When will you…take me?" I asked breathlessly.

My damned stomach rumbled again, ruining the moment. "Soon," he assured me. "First, you need to eat. Then you must rest. You'll need your strength."

And with that, he turned on his heel and left, the door closing behind him. Food was sent to me shortly. Instead of Ayres bringing it as I'd hoped, it was slid through the bottom slat in the door. I sat and ate, fuming at being so callously denied. This was my fantasy, so why couldn't I have any control over it? The Ayres in this Episode didn't show any signs of rage or violence. He was certainly huge and intimidating, but he made me quiver more in anticipation than fear. I napped a little—there not being much else to occupy my time. Later, Gol arrived and took me on another trip to the bathroom. Shortly after, another under-the-door meal arrived, which I figured was probably dinner. I finished my meal and curled up on the hard floor, my mind deep in contemplation.

Would Ayres come back and make wild love to me before I woke up from this Episode? Or would I find myself reviving in a room full of doctors and nurses watching while I gyrated against my pillow? How embarrassing. It's not like it would be the first time.

Just as I was about to drift off into oblivion, I heard a 'Psst!' coming from outside my prison cell. I climbed to my feet and shuffled, blanket and all, over to my door. I saw Lissa's dark head bobbing through the bars across the hall.

"What?" I couldn't quite figure out the role Lissa played in this Episode. Maybe she was a simulation of a friend I'd had before I went crazy?

"Have they explained anything to you?" she asked.

I assumed she had been paired up with an alien warrior as I had. "Yeah."

She cast a discerning eye on me. "You're from Earth, aren't you?"

"Yes. Are you?"

"I am." She visibly gulped. "Mandy, I'm afraid. The man who took me—he's not human. And this game he told me about...we could die!"

She was really taking this stuff seriously. Probably suffering from virgin jitters. "We'll be all right," I told her.

"How will we be all right?" she demanded, sounding near hysterics. "The alien—Oro, is his name—said he would take my virginity. That's if I live long enough."

"Did he say he was coming back tonight?" I asked hopefully. Maybe Ayres would return to me, too.

She appeared irritated by my question. "No, he didn't say. Why aren't you afraid?"

I shrugged even though she wouldn't see it. "I dunno. Doesn't this all seem a little 'out there' to you?"

"You think this isn't happening? That we're imagining it all?"

Well, duh. "Don't you?"

She shook her head. "Maybe. I don't know what's real anymore. I've had…visions…for a long time. As crazy as this sounds, I actually feel like I know Oro. He's been in my life for years—well, in my visions, that is."

"It's been the same with me and Ayres," I admitted. A thought occurred to me. "Hey, were you institutionalized?"

"Like in a crazy house? No way."

I was slightly offended by her obvious repulsion.

"My uncle shipped me off to live in an all-girls

school when I was ten. It was really strict—absolutely no contact with any boys allowed."

What better way to keep her a virgin? "You said your uncle sent you there? What about your parents?"

She took a long time to answer. "They…they're dead. They were murdered when I was little."

Same as my parents. Then my aunt and uncle as well.

Was this some kind of conspiracy? Isolate the victim and ensure she remains a virgin until such a time that her alien warrior could claim her for the game? It all made perfect sense. It would guarantee she remained unspoiled. And if the alien visited just enough to make her appear crackers, then all the better when she did eventually mysteriously disappear. Certifiable virgins—it was genius.

CHAPTER 6

"I'm not crazy," Lissa insisted.

"Yes, you are! It's okay, so am I." The sooner she accepted it, the better.

"If this is all a vision, or a dream, then why does it feel so real?"

"The way I figure it, we've gone completely over the edge. We've slipped into this new reality as a way of coping." After all, I was an expert on crazy.

"Then how are we both having the same vision?" she challenged me.

I smiled smartly. "Easy. You're not really here. You're a figment of my imagination." I tapped the side of my temple with my finger for emphasis.

"I am real. But if what you're saying is true, then you're the one who's not here."

There was just no reasoning with a figment of my imagination. "Whatever. You're having a vision, or I am; either way, it's not happening. You may as well enjoy it."

"Enjoy it! Enjoy being hunted down tomorrow? And if I do survive, I get to be molested by a giant perverted alien?"

"Is Oro hot? Ayres is. I don't know about you, but I plan on taking full advantage of my Episode."

"You really are insane," she informed me.

"Come on! An all-girls school? You must be dying to know what it's like to have a man between your legs."

She blushed beet-red. "A little bit, perhaps. In your visions—Episodes—did you and Ayres ever…do it?"

"Oh yeah. Lots of times. I imagined a whole relationship between us. And then he became all possessive and stuff and tried to kill me."

"He tried to kill you?"

"Well, it was all in my mind. Did Oro ever try to kill you?" I asked.

"No. We did have lots of sex, though." She actually giggled.

"We're still virgins. That thingy the warden-cyborg-dude waved over our bellies confirmed it."

"I wondered what he was doing," Lissa said.

"Apparently, we have to be virgins to play this game."

"Sacrificial virgins." She yawned suddenly. "Oro told me to rest—that I need my strength for tomorrow. That's when they're taking us below."

"To Taleon. Yeah, Ayres told me the same thing. Look, whatever happens, don't worry, okay? It's not real."

She seemed comforted by my reasoning. "All right. Get some rest, Mandy. I'll see you tomorrow."

"It'll be entertaining, I'm sure. Sleep well." I wandered back over to lie down in the middle of the floor again. Tomorrow we would start the game, and then, at night, if Lissa was right, Ayres would claim my virginity—yet again. This time, it would feel completely real. I smiled. Let the games begin.

* * * *

I awoke bright and early the next morning.

At least, I assumed it was morning. The lights had gone out last night just as I was drifting off, and now they were back on again. Like clockwork, Gol arrived to take me to the bathroom and then returned me to my cell. As soon as I settled myself on the floor, I heard a ruckus in the hall. Sounds of many booted feet and the whoosh of doors opening made me jump to my feet. When my door opened, a guard I'd never seen before stood there. He held a bundle in his hands and tossed it at my feet. As I stared down at what appeared to be clothes, he reached down beside the outside wall and pulled a tray of food into the room. He slid it closer to me with his booted foot.

"Eat, dress, and prepare yourself," he said.

I resisted the urge to salute.

As the door closed, I looked down at the tray of food. It actually looked slightly more appetizing this morning. I sat down and ate quickly, being anxious to get dressed. It'd be nice to move around in something other than the stupid blanket. Done with the food, I held up the clothing to inspect. The outfit consisted of two pieces: a shirt and black pants—similar to the ones worn on old episodes of Star Trek. They must have figured I was going to live through the ordeal, considering the shirt was green, not red. They'd also given me socks and a pair of black boots. No panties and no bra. Great. Not that I was top-heavy or anything, but still…

As soon as I finished dressing, the door opened again. The same guy who came earlier was back again. He gestured for me to step out into the hall. We began moving down the passageway. I noticed there were other females being escorted by other guards. Ushered down several more hallways, I was led onto an elevator and was quickly whisked below. The guard, who held my arm now, led me down another maze of corridors until we finally walked through a huge set of double doors into what appeared to be a hangar. Several small spacecraft were parked in a row against the far wall. Down the center of the floor appeared to be a runway, at the end of which was a massive exit I assumed led to outer space. Smug in my assurance that this was all fake, I took in my surroundings with awe and wonder—but not fear. It was as though I'd stepped into a three-dimensional movie, and I got to be the star.

My guard led me over to the far right of the room, where a group was forming. Several young women each stood with a guard beside them. The women displayed a mix of emotions. Some appeared defiant, a few were crying—one being almost hysterical—while others looked so frightened they were about to faint. I was brought into line beside them. They stared at me curiously. I suppose because I wore no emotion except interest. A few minutes later, Lissa was brought up to stand beside me. We nodded at each other and smiled conspiratorially.

The alien warriors filed into the hangar next, each of them giant and rough-looking. They walked over to stand in front of their females, and once they were all in place, the guards relinquished their duties and moved away from us. I noticed they didn't leave the room, rather they stood at intervals around the floor. I assumed in case there was any trouble. I looked up at Ayres and noticed he was dressed all in black.

All of the warriors wore tight-fitting black pants, high leather boots, and V-neck tunics in an array of colors and fabrics that were belted at their waist. Their tunics were short-sleeved, showing off thick arms rippling with large muscles and various tattoos.

Definitely hot.

We continued to stand there, the men on one side, facing the women on the other. I couldn't help but smirk a little.

"Something amuses you?" Ayres asked.

"Looks like we're about to line dance," I replied. When he scowled at me, I shrugged. "I thought you said there was only gonna be five couples competing?"

Ayres gave me a pointed look. "There will be."

"Are we gonna draw straws or do rock, paper, scissors?" I asked.

"No. You will fight," he informed me.

"Say, what?" Surely, I had misheard him.

"You will fight," he repeated, gesturing to an area off to the left that I'd failed to notice earlier. It appeared to resemble a boxing ring.

I gulped. "To...the death?"

"No. First blood. The last five will be allowed to compete." He grilled me with a creepy stare. "Do not fail."

Well, this wasn't any fun at all! I'd had an idea

where this Episode was going, and it was not into a ring, sweating it out with a bunch of scrapping females. It was supposed to be about Ayres and me enjoying crazy, wild sex on the surface of Taleon.

A loud bong sounded, which I presumed was the signal for the fight to begin, since all the warriors grabbed hold of their women and began pulling them toward the ring. Ayres reached for me and began yanking me over as well.

I pulled my hand free of his. "I'm capable of walking," I informed him.

He arched an eyebrow. "I hope you're capable of fighting."

Since this was my dream, I was sure it would work out all right. Perhaps I'd be able to display some great technique in the ring, like leaping ten feet into the air, dazzling my opponents, and having them shrinking in fear.

Ayres grabbed hold of the ropes and separated them so I could step into the ring. The other women—I now counted ten of us—eyed each other warily. They all appeared to be from Earth, and we all compared in shape and size, making it a fair fight. I'd never gone toe to toe with anyone before, and I wondered what it would be like. The warriors all backed away so they couldn't interfere with the battle about to ensue. Then the man with the red shoulders, Baynar, the leader, whom I recognized from yesterday's meeting, came forward and stepped into the middle of the ring.

"This will be a battle to first blood, to determine the five competitors in this season's tournament," he announced. The warrior men looked tense, and I sensed they were concerned that their fate now rested with the women they had snatched. I rolled my shoulders, laced my fingers, and pushed them out to crack my knuckles like a butch. I wasn't too concerned about being one of the remaining five standing. After all, I was in excellent shape. There was a workout room at Lindove that I regularly made use of. I also jogged around the grounds—with an attendant—and Uncle Mick had taught me a few moves in the event I ever needed to defend myself.

Baynar stepped from the ring and dropped his arm. "Begin!"

All the women looked around at each other, not sure how to start. Since this was my Episode, I figured I might as well take the lead. After all, the sooner I got this part out of the way, the sooner I could spend time wrapped in Ayres' arms.

I moved to the center of the ring and swung my gaze around. "Come on," I said, posing jauntily. "Who's first?" I looked over at Ayres and winked.

Lissa came up to me, and we smiled at each other. "A dream, remember?" she said.

"Let's make it a good one," I told her. We stood back to back, facing the women who had half-heartedly begun to push and shove at each other. There was some hair-pulling and name-calling before things began to get serious. A short blonde kicked a brunette in the leg, who, in turn, called her a 'stupid bitch'. That got things rolling.

Soon, we had a full-blown catfight going on. There was screaming and crying, swearing, and a lot of slapping. Anyone who got close enough to Lissa or me got booted or punched. I surprised myself by giving a wild-eyed redhead a wallop in the nose, causing her to squirt blood.

"Oh! Sorry about that," I said while she was pulled from the ring. A couple of guards had climbed over the ropes to referee and escort the losers off. It was several long minutes before there were only five of us standing. Lissa and I turned to each other and smiled. She reached her hand out to my face.

"Oh, you're bleeding!" she said. I guess in the excitement, I hadn't noticed one of the women had scratched me. At least it must have been after I'd gotten her, so I had been allowed to remain.

I touched the scratch gently with my fingers

while the alien warriors shouted and argued, some yelling victoriously. My fingers came away bloodied.

I stared at the blood, not even noticing Ayres until he came up beside me and took my hand, raising my arm up high in the air. The look on his face was triumphant. A drop of blood dripped from my finger and landed at my feet.

What the hell?

With all the excitement over, I began to feel pain. Where I'd been punched in the arm, my skin was becoming purple. My ribs hurt from a lucky shot someone had delivered.

I'd felt pain in an Episode before—especially when I was actually acting it out, yet there had never been any blood. When Ayres and I had had sex for the first time, I knew it was supposed to hurt, and so it had, slightly, but even then, there'd been no blood.

I looked over at the smiling face of Lissa, who had battled alongside me quite brilliantly. The dreamy look she wore made me realize she was still caught up in the notion of this being a vision.

It was then, as I looked around and began to focus on my surroundings, that fear began to envelop me. This wasn't an Episode. Not when I had shed blood.

This was for real.

CHAPTER 7

The man beside me suddenly seemed much more powerful and a heck of a lot larger than he had a few minutes ago. I looked at him with new eyes. Had I actually entertained the idea of having wild sex with that animal? He would break me in half if his heavy body didn't crush me beneath him first. The room began to sway. Voices faded in and out. Faces stretched and then shrank before my eyes while panic took hold of me. I wiggled my toes and clenched and unclenched my fists, trying to get the blood pumping back into my brain. Ayres must have noticed my distress because I soon felt an iron grip on my arm holding me steady.

"What's wrong?" he growled, his voice seeming far away.

Wake up now! Wake up!

"I am not asleep," he said.

Did I say that out loud? Holy shit! I didn't know what was happening anymore. I'd been so in control. So sure I was having an Episode. Jack and Danny at the cabin, those terrible things Ayres had said about Earth, and this bloody catfight came crashing down around me.

It had all been real!

The room began to spin round and round. All my efforts concentrated on holding tight to the giant beside me. The astounding irony of it was that the man I clung to was the person responsible for this situation. Had he existed all along?

"I feel sick," I told him, shutting my eyes tight.

Vaguely, I became aware of someone calling my name. Lissa.

"Is she all right?"

Ayres swung me up into his arms, making my head swim even more. "She'll be fine," I heard him reply.

Jostled, I knew he was probably maneuvering us around the ropes of the ring. Then he was walking briskly. Laughter rang in my ears.

"Not so tough, is she?" someone jibbed. Ayres didn't reply, but I could feel his arms tighten around me.

We soon came to a halt, and Ayres bent and set me down onto something soft. I chanced a peek—and seeing the room no longer spun—kept my eyes open. Ayres knelt down and stared at me angrily.

"What is wrong with you?"

What could I say? All this time I thought I was

crazy, but—lucky me—I'm not? His deep blue eyes were as cold as ice. His body seemed clenched in anticipation. He had a lot at stake in this tournament, he'd said. And apparently, if I couldn't participate, he couldn't either. I didn't fool myself into thinking he actually cared for me. I was merely a pawn in his game, a means to an end.

When I remained silent, he scowled more. "Can you continue?"

What would he do if I said no? Looking around the hangar, I noticed the losers had made themselves scarce. What would happen to those poor, unfortunate women who must contend with their pissed-off alien partners who'd hoped to compete?

I nodded my head, bringing a grunt of relief from the man before me. "What happens now?" I managed to ask.

"We will go below to Taleon." He didn't seem concerned that we'd soon be on a strange planet battling for our lives. The only thing I had going for me was that in order to win, he'd have to keep me alive. My gaze shot to Lissa, who was standing proudly beside Oro. She was smiling, the poor misbegotten fool. She still thought this was fake, thanks to yours truly. Perhaps it'd be better that way. If she knew the truth, she'd be as batty as I was. I wondered what would happen if she and Oro lost. She'd be left behind on Taleon forever. How precious would she be to Oro then? Would he become her worst nightmare? That was, if she even survived. This could be my fate as well. Despite the confidence my companion displayed, there were no guarantees we'd be successful either. I couldn't imagine being doomed to spend my life with Ayres. If I thought he was scary in my Episodes, I could well imagine his ire in reality.

"You need to rise." Ayres was looking around, and I, too, became aware of the stares and comments being directed our way. Appearances were paramount. If I looked weak or ill, the other competitors may come for me first. With his help, I was able to get to my feet. I took a couple of assisted steps before I felt steady enough to not require his aid.

Ayres led me over to a raised circular platform where the other pairs were now gathering. The teams took up position around the outer edges, forming a circle with us facing each other. The competition appeared tough—not the females, who were all about my size, but their alien warriors. I stole a glance at Ayres, who stood straight and proud at my side. He was as formidable as any of the other men, perhaps more so.

"Aren't we getting into a ship?" I whispered.

"No." He frowned and replied without looking at me.

"Then how are we supposed to get to the surface..." My voice trailed off when I saw a beam of white light come from above. It grew in size, creeping steadily across the surface of the platform. One by one, the contestants began to evaporate before my eyes as the light washed over them. "Shit!" Ayres seized my arm when he saw me begin to back away. And then the light was upon us. The very light I recognized from the times I'd seen it at the cottage. There was no time to think or react. One moment I was on the ship, and then—poof—I was no more.

Next thing I knew, I was whirling through space, my body becoming a zillion particles. I had no eyeballs, yet I could see myself—or at least I was aware of myself—scattered about. A cluster of little throbbing lights comprised my whole being. Other clusters floated around me in the darkness, along with great swirls of colors. We were moving without thought or effort, guided by some unseen force. As quickly as I'd vanished, I unscrambled and became whole again, arrived now in another place.

Looking about in stunned silence, I noticed Ayres on my left. Strange that although we'd just been particles of light, I had felt his presence, known him even, distinguishing him from the others. He turned his gaze on me, and I suddenly became grateful for his company. He was my constant in this topsy-turvy chain of events.

"Are you all right?" he asked.

I looked down at my body, and everything appeared to be in the proper place. "I believe so." Discussing what had just happened seemed futile. While it was strange to have experienced beaming around firsthand, I'd seen it happen many times on Star Trek.

"What the fuck was that!" I heard a woman exclaim. Across from us, I saw her, on her knees, sucking in deep breaths of air. Her alien stood over her, frowning and glancing around at the other participants. Lissa and I exchanged a look, and with relief, I could see she remained unconcerned.

"Rise," the woman's partner told her impatiently.

"Fuck you!" she screamed, becoming completely out of control. "What is going on? I didn't agree to this. None of us have." She looked around at the other females, hands outstretched. "Did we?" she demanded when a few of them ignored her and turned away.

"Be silent!" her alien ordered.

Not to be denied her moment, the woman leaped to her feet and faced off against the giant, snarling beast before her. She actually poked her finger into his chest. "Don't you order me. I've had enough of this bullshit. You took me from my home, then had me locked in a cell for days, then told—not asked—but told me about some stupid tournament I had to participate in."

The look on the alien's face really freaked me out. He suddenly reached out and grabbed the woman by her throat with one hand. He then proceeded to pick her up off the ground until she was eye level with him. Horrible choking noises came from her mouth. Her eyes bulged in terror. When I would have leaped forward to help her, Ayres threw a restraining arm in front of me.

"Do not interfere," he snapped, his voice devoid of emotion.

"But..."

He glared down at me and stood firm.

In helpless anger, I watched as the poor woman became blue in the face. Her body twitched a few times and then went slack. The alien dropped her to the ground, where she lay at his feet like a piece of baggage. He pushed at her still form with his boot, and when she failed to stir, he actually shrugged his shoulders. Then he looked around at the other contestants. "There is always next year," he said. He tapped on a black button in the center of a silver band wrapped around his wrist.

"I withdraw," he said. "Return me." A moment later, he and the woman dissolved into a cluster of throbbing lights—beamed away—back to the ship, I presume.

Mouth hanging open, I stared at the spot where they had been, before my eyes snapped back to Ayres. "I thought we were stuck here if we didn't win." I don't know why that was my first reaction to the scene I'd just witnessed.

"The game has not officially begun. There is time to forfeit."

Looking at the same band Ayres sported on his wrist, I said, "Maybe we should as well." None of us women got to have a band.

"No," Ayres determined. "We will win, or we will die."

Those were some choices. Looking around at the shocked and defeated faces of the other women—except poor delusional Lissa—I had the feeling I had no other choice but to go on. Or else…

CHAPTER 8

So now the moment was upon us. We were set to begin. A loud horn sounded—coming from God knows where—making the aliens leap to attention and begin to guide their females to the appointed starting position. There was an actual line drawn in the sand. My gaze swept the vast landscape as I took my first serious look at Planet Taleon. If I weren't scared shitless, I would describe the scene before me as beautiful. Definitely alien, but beautiful all the same. Three giant moons crested the deep blue sky, while fluffy white clouds floated gently about. Miles of reddish sand stretched out before us. Throughout the desert, colossal, haphazard piles of stones jutted upward. Beyond the sand was a mammoth jungle resembling pictures I'd seen of tropical rainforests. Enormous green velvet mountains soared as far as the eye could see. The air was fresh and sweet-smelling, untainted by pollution, making my lungs expand greedily with each breath I took. I felt Ayres' eyes upon me. Looking up at his grim face, I sensed that despite the calm scenery surrounding us, we would face a world of threats.

"Stay by my side," he told me. As if I had a choice. I was no fool. The other females remained close to their partners, eyeing the other aliens with wary, watchful eyes. The couples around us were soon to become our combatants, and I, too, looked upon them with a calculated, assessing gaze. Who would be the first to fall, I wondered? Who would be victorious and who would be left here to rot?

From the corner of my eye, I caught a flash of movement to my left. Fearfully, I watched as a four-legged spider-like robot crept toward the line, its pointy legs stabbing at the sand with each step it took. Atop the metal frame sat an upright screen about two feet wide by two feet high. The robot came to rest at the center of our group, and suddenly the screen switched on, and a man became visible—Baynar. His voice crackled for a moment and then became clear.

"Challengers," he addressed us. "Your odds have increased as Daleon has forfeited. I trust the four remaining teams will prevail and do Calixtus proud. Show us your strength and skills as noble warriors as you strive to reach the end. As you know, there can be only one victorious pair. The winner will be granted his boon. The losers will remain on Taleon to live out the rest of their days. Beware warriors. Those former players left to the mercy of this planet are now your enemies." The screen zoomed back to give a full view of the room Baynar was in. Behind him were the other members of the council I'd seen on the deck of the ship. Baynar raised his hand. "Remember. We will be with you every step of your journey." Whether that was meant as an implied threat or friendly encouragement, I had no idea. I knew all eyes of Calixtus would be watching the event unfold.

"Each of you has already selected your preferred weapon," Baynar continued. "Be careful with it. You will not be given another." With a nod of his head, weapons suddenly materialized in front of us in a neat line. The warriors stepped forward and picked them up. Ayres held a deadly-looking long metal staff resembling a double-sided scythe that glimmered as the sun struck it. The other three warriors had chosen metal medieval-like weapons; each of them would be lethal in the right hands.

I noticed the females hadn't been given any weapons. When I remarked on this, Ayres smiled tolerantly as though I were a dolt. "You would have difficulty lifting any of the weapons here, and you would not know how to wield them."

"Give me a .45 automatic, buddy, and ask me where your balls are." Not an idle threat, I rationalized. Uncle Mick had been a marksman and had taught me how to shoot.

Ayres wasn't impressed.

The speaker crackled, and all eyes snapped to the screen. "Once again, good luck to you all. And may Tanit watch over you." The screen went blank, and the spider-robot crept away.

"Who's Tanit?" I asked, figuring it was perhaps a god or goddess of Calixtus.

He gave me another 'you're a dolt' look and didn't bother to respond to my question. All his attention now seemed focused intently on the tournament. He appeared drawn as tight as a bowstring, his hands holding the metal scythe in a death grip. My sweeping glance took in the other contestants. The alien-warriors all stood alert and eager.

"Get ready," Ayres said. His weapon fit nicely onto his back in a harness-like contraption he strapped on, leaving his hands free. He reached out and laced his fingers through mine, then bent down and shifted his stance as though about to start a race.

"Oh, shit."

The loud horn sounded once more, and everyone took off. Ayres moved so fast he practically dragged me behind him. Instead of slowing down, he swept me up over his shoulder in one fluid motion. My head jostled against his back beside his weapon, which he wore diagonally across his other shoulder. At least I had no worries of the sharp blades cutting into me. Lifting my head, I saw that along with Ayres and me, one other couple had also darted off and continued to barrel toward the sanctuary of the jungle. The other two couples had stopped soon after take-off. Now they appeared to be battling. From my precarious position, I saw flashing white and red lights that looked to be coming from the aliens' weapons. I could hear screaming, too, growing fainter and fainter with every stride Ayres took. I was glad to see Oro and Lissa were the other couple that had run off like we had. A glimpse of bouncing black curls over Oro's back confirmed it. I guess Lissa's alien thought she ran too slow as well.

Ayres didn't slow down until we reached the jungle. Even then, he dodged, leaped, and ducked the many obstacles he encountered while still maintaining a swift jog. Finally, he slowed enough to swing me to my feet. He kept hold of my hand and tugged me along, keeping to his pace. I knew this was mainly a race to the finish line. Ayres had said we'd be here for a week, and I hoped he didn't plan on running the entire time.

A few minutes later, he finally slowed right down and then stopped. I noticed he'd barely broken a sweat, and his breath was steady. I was puffing like a locomotive and had to lean against a tree for support. Ayres began grabbing at vines and fastening the ends together.

"What're you doing?"

"Slowing down the others," he answered. "We must all keep to the same route. Not the same trails exactly, but the way is laid out. They will be close." He cocked his head and listened. "We must hurry."

He'd fashioned the vines into a crude rope across the trail we were on. The ends still hung high from the treetops. It was clear that anyone coming this way would see the barrier and simply go under or over it. Ayres pulled the scythe off his back and aimed it up high at one end of the vine. I jumped when a dart of green light flashed out of the end of it and hit a heavy limb dead center, leaving a black scorch mark. I'd seen marks like that before—on the cottage door. The limb cracked and fell slightly, but remained where it was.

"Come," he said. I realized that if anyone touched the vine even slightly, the branch would swing down in a deadly arc and land right in the pathway—and into anyone unfortunate enough to be standing there. I suppose I should have been impressed, but I shivered and felt slightly sick instead. The reality of the game had set in. Here we were going to have to do things—uncomfortable things—and make life and death decisions. It was clear Ayres played to win, and if anyone got in his way, he would fight and possibly kill. I didn't relish the idea. The cruel Kale of my Episodes was but a pale shade in comparison to the machine that marched me through the jungle. I shivered again and hurried to catch up. Machine or not, he was the only thing standing between me and death.

We marched for hours, it seemed, pausing only when Ayres deemed it safe to rest for a moment or two. We'd been given no provisions, but along our journey, I could see the trail was ripe with an abundance of fresh fruits—weird-looking, but tasty—and several small running streams to provide drinking water. Ayres seemed knowledgeable about what was good to eat and drink and what was not. When I snagged a purple plum-like piece of fruit off a tangle of short, wiry bushes, he smacked it from my hand before I could pop it in my mouth.

"You will writhe like a snake, foam at the mouth, and die within five Earth minutes if you eat that," he informed me.

"Well, thanks," I said sarcastically.

The jungle went on forever. I'd never actually been in a real jungle before, but this one was similar in many ways to pictures and movies I'd seen, to what

I'd expect to find on Earth. Except for those giant ever-present moons in the sky, I almost felt I was on Earth. Where were all the dangers we'd been warned about? There'd been no sign of dangerous wildlife or Varlings anywhere. In fact, everything was unnaturally silent. There were some strange-looking birds squawking and chirping, but those were the only living things I'd laid eyes upon up to this point.

Ayres stopped suddenly, and since I was looking up, I ran right into his back. He didn't seem to notice. His head was cocked at an angle again, so I figured he was listening to something. Whatever it was, I had no idea—I couldn't hear anything unusual.

He reached back suddenly and pulled me off the trail several yards, and then stopped to lean against the trunk of a thick tree. Strong arms wrapped around me and held me so that my back rested against a mass of chest muscles. I became acutely aware of the heat of the body I was pressed against. I stayed still and silent, part of me enjoying the contact.

A rustling sound came from the trail, followed by heavy footsteps and a great sigh. "How much further?" asked a female with a whiny voice.

"Silence," her companion warned her. It was several minutes later before the footsteps faded away, and Ayres deemed it safe to return to the trail. I guess they'd managed to avoid Ayres' swinging limb of death.

To keep the tedium at bay, I began to badger Ayres with questions. He indulged my curiosity with cryptic answers as long as I spoke to him in whispers. Conversing like this, I had to keep close beside him.

"Do you know what happened to those guys at the cottage?" He'd supplied all the answers to various questions about Taleon and the tournament. This question, however, was a tough one. Part of me wanted to know, while another part of me didn't. When Ayres didn't answer right away, I elaborated. "You know, the ones in white coats I was with? There was this beam of light coming out of the bedroom, and Danny got sucked right in. I dunno where Jack..."

"They're on the ship."

"Come again?"

"They are on the ship," he said with slow pronunciation.

Relief flooded me. "So, they're alive?"

He smirked. "We do not make a habit of transporting the dead."

"What are you going to do with them?"

"If you had refused to participate in the tournament, I would have used them to coerce your assent."

Since I'd thought this entire affair was a coma-induced nightmare, it hadn't been necessary. No. I'd strolled down this path to hell all on my own.

CHAPTER 9

"What will you do with them now?" I asked.

"Depends," Ayres replied.

He was exasperating. "Depends on what?"

"If we lose and must remain here, their fate will not be ours to decide."

"And if we win?"

He pondered for a moment. "Then I shall grant you a boon. If you wish them returned to Earth, then I shall have it arranged."

"How generous." Considering he'd taken them in the first place, I didn't bother to hide my sarcasm. "Just how long have you been planning for me to be in this tournament?" Since we were laying our cards on the table, I wanted to know if he and his kind were responsible for things that had happened to me and my family. Could it be possible he'd had his eye on me ever since I was a child? My parents had died under mysterious circumstances, making my aunt and uncle my guardians before I'd even turned three. Then they had been killed. I remembered that Event. Weird things had occurred, such as tremors and bright lights.

Ayres stopped suddenly and faced me. "There are things you do not know. Those people you called family—they're not what they seemed to be."

"What? What do you mean?"

"Some people on Earth are actually from Calixtus. They make their living seeking out recruits, young females and sometimes males, to be used in tournaments, selling them off to the highest bidder. I had nothing to do with you being chosen." He sounded defensive.

"Are you saying my aunt and uncle were from Calixtus?" No frigging way.

"Your aunt, yes, your uncle, no. He had no idea. They rarely do. The Trackers—as they are called—are masters at infiltration and manipulation. Your parents were disposed of when you were young." It wasn't a question, but a fact. "She would have been responsible for that."

My legs felt shaky all of a sudden, and I moved off the trail to sit down on a moss-covered rock. Ayres came and stood by me, his eyes shifting about the area, always on guard. If he saw from my expression that he'd revealed too much information, he didn't let it stop him from continuing.

"You had been set in place for another."

I stared at him as if he'd grown another head.

What did he mean? Another alien?

He nodded his head at my unvoiced question. "Another meant to take you, but I intercepted. There was a battle and…"

"And my uncle was killed in the crossfire?"

"Yes. It was unfortunate, and I didn't mean for it to happen that way. It was not me who killed him. It was she."

"Aunt Erin killed my Uncle Mick?"

"Yes. And she would have killed you, too, but I didn't allow it. She would rather have seen you dead than to have me mark you for my own." He looked away.

"Who was I meant for?" Did it really matter? Whether I'd been marked for Ayres or some other alien, I was still nothing more than a plaything to be used. All for a stupid game.

Ayres didn't answer, and when I glared at him, he finally faced me. "My brother."

"Your brother?"

"But when he got into trouble, you were put back onto the block, and the highest bidder was the one who had the right to claim you."

So I was bartered and bid on, all without my knowledge. It took me a moment to control my fury. Ayres didn't seem to notice the inner battle that raged within me.

"My brother owed a great deal of money. He figured he could enter the tournament with you, win, and then be granted a boon of forgiveness of the debt. But you were too young, and he'd run out of time. He decided to clear his debt in another way and, unfortunately, got himself into more trouble. He was incarcerated on Drone—Calixtus' fourth moon—and will soon face death."

"So you intercepted me and decided to play for his life?"

"Yes. It cost me a great deal of money to secure you. But the Tracker—your 'aunt', had a personal vendetta against Kenix, my brother. She was furious when I told her my plans. That is why she wanted you dead."

"Is this the part when I'm supposed to thank you for my life?" I stood up and began to pace. "According to you, Calixtus has used Earth since the beginning of time. Not just our planet but our people as well. We're nothing more to you than game pieces. Never mind that we have lives of our own."

He shrugged. "It is the way things have always been. We need to keep moving." He gestured for me to come with him. I had no choice but to follow.

I watched his back for a while along the

pathway. The weird birds continued to shrill, oblivious to our presence. "You know I've seen you since I was sixteen."

"I know."

"Weren't you concerned that your future partner was crazy? You know, I was put in an asylum after the hell I went through at the cottage."

"You're not crazy. A little disturbed after what happened, perhaps, which is only natural for a frail woman."

"Wow, all this flattery is gonna go to my head. And I am crazy. I saw you a lot, had realistic episodes of a life we had together, and everything." I wasn't about to tell him about the wild sex or how he'd gone postal.

"It's not your fault. It is the device in your head."

I stopped walking. It took him a moment to notice before he stopped as well and turned around. "What device?"

"An implant. So I could keep track of you. Sometimes it messes with the mind. It's all right. The device was turned off once I took you."

"You put an alien implant in me that made me nuts?" What a fucking asshole.

"Yes. I had to make sure I could find you when the time came."

"This just keeps getting better and better."

It seemed my whole life was a lie. I'd been nothing but a hostage, really, to the whims of Calixtus. Every major event had been controlled and manipulated by an alien race waiting to claim me. Though it hadn't been Ayres at first, he'd been the one to take his brother's place, and he'd even implanted me—made me think I was insane. Images of Aunt Erin flashed in my mind. I'd always wondered why I'd catch her watching me sometimes with a strange look in her eye, a look I now figured was calculation.

"Why did my aunt—or whoever she was—have it out for your brother?" I asked. Ayres slowed so that I could keep pace with him. "Didn't she find me and spend years pretending to be something she wasn't, all for him? Or was it about the money?"

"She did what she did, not just for the money Kenix gave her, but because she loved him. He cared for her, but he did not share her infatuation. When he went to prison, she was furious. I saw him on Drone and he told me about you and what he'd planned to do originally. He wasn't sure how Vara—the Tracker—would handle things. I discovered that she had put you on the block after Kenix was imprisoned. I was able to purchase you from that warrior." When he saw he had my undivided attention, he continued.

"When I went to let Vara know you were now meant for me, and how I planned to use you to help me free Kenix, she grew irrational. She wanted revenge on Kenix. She'd given up years of her life for him, she said, and all for nothing. That he would foolishly risk everything and wind up on Drone anyway told her that she meant nothing to him. So at the cabin, she tried to kill me."

"Why don't I remember any of this?"

"Vara stunned you and your uncle just before I arrived. She thought it was the other warrior coming to claim you. We battled, and she and your uncle were killed. I was wounded, and I had to return to Calixtus. Before I left, I implanted you."

"It took me three days to wake up. They found me surrounded by body parts." Thank God I didn't remember seeing that.

"As it was, you were still too young for the tournament. I had to wait until you were twenty Earth years—part of the rules. A good thing the judicial system on Drone takes so long to carry out a sentence."

In some twisted way, I could relate to Ayres' logic. He was driven by the need to save his brother. Although it didn't excuse what had happened to me, nor what his people did to mine.

CHAPTER 10

Night was falling, and everything around us took on a shadowy, sinister tinge. What had seemed beautiful and calm in the daylight hours now became creepy and dangerous. Our day of trudging had been uneventful, and except for the couple we'd seen earlier, no one had crossed our path.

When Ayres showed no signs of slowing down, I glared at his back. "How much further?"

"One hundred of your Earth miles."

I halted in my tracks. "Say what?" He couldn't possibly be serious. He stopped and turned around. With a great sigh, I continued walking.

"From start to finish, we will travel one hundred miles," he clarified.

"In one week?" He nodded. "How much further do we have to walk today?"

"Do you grow tired?"

More like exhausted. It didn't help that the fruit he'd been feeding me had cramped up my belly, and I'd had to dive into the bushes every hour or so. He'd complained about the delay, which was no doubt why he drove us on relentlessly. "Yes, I'm tired."

Without losing pace, he swung me up into his arms, carrying me like a baby. "Rest," he said.

The heat of his body against the cool night air, and the lull of his swaggering steps, soon had me resting my head on his chest. The real-life him was so different from my Episodes. His scent was more masculine and his muscles more firm. Seeing the brightest moon reflect off the deadly blade of his scythe, I felt protected. I didn't fool myself into thinking Ayres felt anything for me other than the necessity to keep me alive so he could win the game. Despite him being in my life for the past four years, it had been one-sided. He may have popped in once in a while, but he'd explained to me that images of him were programmed into the implant, so when the time came for him to come for me, I would know him. And he'd been right. When he'd reached out his hand to me at the cottage, I'd clung to him like a rope in quicksand.

I dreamt. Swirling images of spaceships, slashing scythes, moons—and Uncle Mick lying in a pool of blood at my feet. Whenever sadness and restlessness overcame me, a voice reached out to me in the darkness. "Shhh, you're all right," it soothed, allowing me to drift away to dream of comforting caresses and kisses. I awoke suddenly when my ass hit the ground with a thump. Brain fog and the dark night sky distorted my vision.

"I have already lost," yelled a voice. "But I will make sure you do not succeed."

Bolts of colored laser light zoomed back and forth between two giant male forms, yielding their weapons. I recognized one of the men as Ayres. The lights flew wild, hitting branches and making sickening cracking noises. A crash sounded close to my right, making me leap to my feet in fear. I saw the snarling face of one of the alien warriors turn to me and grin sadistically.

"Fear not, girl. I will make it quick," he said.

In a brief instant, Ayres' gaze locked with mine. I froze. "Run!" he yelled. Needing no further encouragement, I scrambled into the brush and ducked down out of sight. Letting loose a battle cry that made my hair stand on end, Ayres charged forward. Swinging his scythe in a deadly arc, he engaged his opponent, who raised his own weapon in defense.

The man Ayres fought was not Oro, which brought me some comfort. That meant Lissa may still be alive—for now. What would happen, I wondered, if we came face to face with them? Would I have to stand by and watch Ayres kill my friend? Or would Lissa have to watch Oro kill me? Maybe then she'd figure out this was for real.

The battle raged for some time. Both of the men were of a similar size and strength, so it would boil down to skill. Though Ayres had not originally planned to compete in the tournament, he'd had four years to prepare himself. But would it be enough?

Loud shrieks suddenly came from every direction. The jungle appeared to come alive as dark shapes writhed and whirled through the night. Masses of them—whatever they were—grouped together forming a large circle around the two battling men. Deeper into the bushes I scurried, peeking out through the thick tangled vines at the scene less than forty feet away.

The two warriors ceased their fight, and with an exchanged glance, the mortal enemies turned back-to-back to greet their foe. Those twisted, painted bodies, bearing crude weapons, and snarls on their faces, must be the Varlings. Their sheer number gave them an advantage. One on one against an alien warrior, they would not have stood a chance. Even from my vantage point, I could see the gaunt faces and protruding ribs curved around indented bellies.

Ayres took a few steps and held up his scythe in warning. The other warrior, brandishing a deadly-looking broad sword, did the same. "Flee or die where you stand," Ayres threatened.

"Bloody cannibals," the other warrior growled.

Cannibals?

One of the Varlings—I assume the leader—wearing more paint than the others, yelled something I couldn't understand. When he waved his right arm over his head, half the group charged the warriors. Weapons cut and sliced in a blur of speed, and bolts of lasers whirled. Screams mixed with battle cries amid a mass of tangled limbs. The carnage continued until I could take no more. Like a coward, I closed my eyes and put my hands up over my ears. When it finally grew silent, except for the moans of the dying, I dared to look. Ayres and the other warrior remained standing. Both were covered in blood, be it their own or their attackers', I didn't know.

Ayres repeated his threat. "Flee…or die!" I, for one, would have run for the hills.

Eyes locked upon one another—invading aliens, and defending natives. The leader of the Varlings finally dropped his gaze. After muttering a few commands, he and his remaining tribe backed away. They'd suffered enough loss for one day.

Sudden sadness enveloped me as I watched them go, shoulders slumped in defeat. They were no match for the aliens or their weapons. They hadn't stood a chance. Primitive Earthlings probably faced the same fate when invaders from Calixtus had arrived to play their precious games. The future of Teleon could very well be slated for the same fate as Earth. Aliens would be stranded, left behind for generations, thereby forming a new race of inhabitants—people who would grow and adapt and increase in numbers, progressing until Taleon no longer served its purpose. Calixtus would then set out for greener pastures, moving throughout the galaxy, leaving behind misbegotten legacies in their wake.

The two warriors turned to face each other. Both appeared exhausted. Now that their mutual enemy had retreated, they were once again on opposite sides.

"Have done with your fight," Ayres said.

The other man raised up his sword. "I will not be left behind. I would rather die a warrior than be forced into a life of scavenging amongst a bunch of heathens."

"Others are here. Our kind. Find them and make a new life," Ayres suggested. He spoke kindly but still held his weapon ready.

Tension crackled in the air. I held my breath as the two men continued to size each other up. Slowly, the other warrior lowered his sword. Ayres did likewise, but kept his eyes upon him. "Keep your woman close," the man threatened. "If I see you again, I will kill you both." Backing away, he got to the edge of the thick brush and then disappeared. Ayres remained still for some time and then gestured for me to come to him.

The sight of him up close assured me the majority of the blood he wore wasn't his own. He had a few minor scratches, but nothing more serious. I followed him as he went to the small trickling stream and cleaned himself up. Sitting back on the mossy bank, a slight movement caught my eye. A bubble floated close by, no larger than my fist. It bobbed just over my head, and when I reached out to poke it, it bounced off my finger.

"What is that?" As I spoke, I saw another bubble glide gracefully by.

Sitting back on his haunches, his face and chest gleaming with drops of moisture, Ayres noted the strange anomaly. He ran a hand over the top of his dark, brush-cut hair and grinned at me. "Have you not noticed them before now?"

"Them? The bubbles?"

"They are Seers; the eyes and ears of Calixtus. For all who watch the tournament."

"Oh, like little viewer cameras. How clever." I poked at a third bubble drifting by my nose. "And tough little buggers."

"The battle must have drawn their attention.

They will move off soon."

"So are they watching us…all the time?" Those several trips I'd taken into the bushes rose up in my mind.

"Not always. They are mostly around to capture combat moments."

I wondered if they had gathered around, floating intently by as that warrior's partner had been killed? Ayres shifted to sit down beside me, so close that our thighs were touching. When our eyes met, I could see his were shining with intention.

"What?" I stirred uncomfortably under his scrutiny.

"The other warrior most likely did not consummate his partnership before his woman was killed."

"So…" I wasn't sure what he was getting at, but a slight tremor went through me when he put his arm around me to pull me closer.

"I will not make the same mistake."

CHAPTER 11

Did he mean to take me then? Here, by the side of the creek, after what had just occurred? What if the Varlings or that other warrior came back? And besides all that, I couldn't just do it. Not outside. My first time should be special…romantic…and in a bed.

It was plain Ayres had no such qualms. He lowered his head and kissed me. His hand on my back came up to hold my head in place. When I opened my mouth to protest, his tongue shot inside. Gradually, I relaxed. My first real kiss. Nice. I could do this. The kissing part at least. I leaned into him, my body turning so my arms could come up around his neck. The pressure of his lips and the thrust of his tongue became fiercer. This was no sweet young man charming his lover with the promise of delight. No, this man would bend me to his will. Or break me. I gasped when his other hand squeezed my tit and pinched my nipple.

"Whoa there, big fella." I lowered my arms and squirmed away. Before I could go further, his hand darted out and grabbed hold of mine.

"We will join tonight," he informed me.

"I'm really not in the mood. Besides, aren't you tired?" He was pulling me closer, the moss allowing my backside to slide along freely. I tried to pull my hand free, but his hold was tight. Once he got me close enough, he lowered me onto my back. Then he rolled on top of me and pushed my legs apart with one of his. Bracing himself on an elbow, he held most of his weight off of me. His other hand lingered down my body to squeeze my tit again. "Get off!"

Instead of speaking, he kissed me again, yet not so aggressively as the first time. The feel and the scent of him began to battle away at my defenses. His caress was gentle, and as his hand slipped beneath the fabric of my shirt, I was pleasantly surprised when I felt his skin hot against mine. He sat up suddenly, between my thighs. His chest was a mass of rippling muscles and faint scars. A warrior's body. My eyes drank in the sight of him, mesmerized. I barely noticed when he lifted my shirt and pulled it off over my head. I remembered I wasn't wearing a bra. Or panties. He snatched my hands as I tried to cover my boobs. He lowered his body and kissed me again, while his rock-hard erection pressed against my leg.

A thought dawned on me. "Aren't I supposed to be a virgin for the game?" I mumbled against his lips.

"At the beginning of the tournament, you must be free of a man's touch." His lips moved on to my neck and then began to trail lower.

"So, why's it okay to do it now?"

He paused just over my nipple, the warmth of his breath making it pebble. "There is a legend. I believe it goes back to the days of old, when the tournaments just began. The women chosen by their warriors could be anyone. Some warriors chose strong, fierce warrior women to fight by their side, while others brought their mates. The story goes that one of the women who entered the game was with child. She was killed by another competitor. Her mate demanded blood rites from the warrior who had killed her. It is law on Calixtus that anyone who kills a child shall be executed. The warrior, who had killed the pregnant woman, ultimately won the game with his mate. He was granted a boon—his life. But after discovering his crime—for he had not known the other woman was with child—the warrior, overcome with remorse, asked that his boon instead be granted that any woman who shall enter the game must be untouched, so that his crime would never be repeated."

"What happened to him?" I asked.

"The warrior was granted his boon. He was brought back down to Earth—where the game was said to be first played—and the pregnant woman's mate, who had been left behind, killed him.

"Wow. He had the rules of the game changed at the cost of his life."

"Yes," Ayres said. "Does that answer your question?"

"I guess. But what if me or one of the other women are impregnated here, during the game?" It was a possibility.

"We have come a long way since those early days," he informed me. "One Earth month before the tournament begins, the warriors are given an injection to prevent the chance of conception. It will be effective for several Earth months. The women are checked just before the game to ensure that they are untouched."

"Well, that's clever."

He grinned at me wolfishly. "So you see? There is nothing to worry about." Lowering his head, he fastened onto my nipple. My back arched as I felt the nip of his teeth. I held his head in my hands, watching him in the darkness. He sat up and then rose to his feet to remove his boots and pants. Then he knelt at my feet and took off my boots. With a firm grip on the bottom of my pants, he whisked them off and tossed them aside.

Now we were both completely naked.

Before I could cross my legs or try to wiggle into a modest pose, he was on the ground between my legs again. As he lowered, I'd caught sight of his cock. It was erect and enormous. And now it was seeking entry into my body.

"Ayres, don't…I'm not ready."

Despite his hot kisses, my body felt more anxiety than anticipation. This would be the first time we'd really made love. I'd longed for him to take me on the ship—back when I'd foolishly believed this was all an Episode. Now I wasn't so brave.

Ayres began kissing a trail down my body. Starting at my collarbone and working his way to my belly. His hands held my breasts and gently massaged, pinching my nipples into tight little buds. As his head dipped lower, his hands moved to hold my hips. Soon, I felt his warm breath against my core. His tongue flicked out and licked my other little bud, which had grown taut. He stroked me with his tongue until I felt myself begin to relax and become warm again. My legs opened wider to accommodate him. As his tongue dipped deep inside of me, I could feel the rough whiskers of his cheeks chafe at my thighs. Sensual, it aroused me. His tongue returned to lick at my clit, and I felt one large finger slip into my passage. Then another. Gently, he pushed deep inside me, only to pull back out and then push inside again.

My head sashayed from side to side while I reached down to grab hold of his ears, urging him deeper…deeper. "Please!" I cried, unashamed of the force of my need. Every sex Episode I'd had with him hadn't even come close to this.

Taking mercy on me, Ayres began kissing his way back up my body. I reached down and took hold of his cock. Soon, this would be inside me. A shiver of fear tore through me again. He was so strong, so large. Would it hurt?

I guided his cock to my opening and let go of him to brace my hands on his chest. As he surged forward in one powerful thrust, I grabbed hold of his shoulders and hung on for dear life. His lips crushed against mine, capturing my cry. He paused for a moment, letting me adjust to his size, and then he began to move. Slowly at first, plunging deep and withdrawing, as he'd done with his fingers. Faster he began to stroke, until I became a mindless frenzy of want and desire. My hips arched up to meet his thrusts. I was no longer mindful of the ground beneath my ass or the chill of the night air as a sheen of sweat covered our bodies. All I saw was the stars overhead twinkling brightly. They seemed to dance more frantically as my world suddenly burst. I cried out and buried my face against

Ayres' chest. He drove into me a couple more times, and one last time, before he stilled. He didn't throw back his head or cry out as I had. Instead, he stared me straight in the eyes. They gleamed in the moonlight, fierce and primitive.

"Mine," he said.

"Yes." What else could I do in that moment when I had been so utterly claimed but agree?

CHAPTER 12

I woke up alone. Sometime during the night, I'd shoved my clothing beneath me, trying to ward off the dampness of the spongy moss. It'd made a soft bed, but as the cool night air mixed with the heat of the ground, it'd become dewy. Ayres had slumbered beside me, the warmth of his body cozy against my exposed skin. His breath had been deep and even, but I'd known he'd awaken at even the slightest noise. Always the warrior.

The babbling creek refreshed me. I crept in slowly, adjusting to the coolness, and bathed as best I could in the two-foot depth. Wet, I emerged and saw Ayres coming up alongside the water's edge, carrying a large fish—I think—in his hands.

As I huddled into my clothes, he knelt and built a small fire. "Hungry?" he asked.

"Yes." The fish was weird-looking, but at least we wouldn't be dining on fruit again.

While he cooked, Ayres peered at me, his gaze seeming to ask a question. Are you all right? Now, in the light of day, recalling how I'd brazenly succumbed to his desire last night, I felt suddenly shy. He'd been rough, yet tender as well, and I'd caught a glimpse of the man he was when he let his guard slip. Perhaps he was not so cool and uncaring toward me after all?

Sitting side by side, we ate. When he finished, he brushed his hands off on his pants and rose to his feet. "We need to get moving," he said. I finished off the last of the pinkish meat he'd given me and got to my feet.

We journeyed on, keeping to the path through the jungle, the cries and chirps of the birds echoing around us. A slight rain began. The winding branches of the tall, thick trees formed a canopy overhead, shielding us effectively. Ayres kept silent, his ever-roving gaze busy keeping watch on our surroundings.

I felt changed. No longer an innocent woman. The ache between my legs and the shiver that shot through me whenever I recalled Ayres' touch reminded me of this fact. Watching his back as I trailed him, I wondered if he was thinking about last night. Probably not. If anything, he most likely itched for another battle. When all of this was over, I questioned if I'd ever see him again. If we lost and had to remain here, he might be so pissed off that he would take his anger out on me. Perhaps he'd chase me off and let me fend for myself? But if we won, and he was granted his boon, and Jack and Danny were released as he'd promised, would he return me to Earth as well? That is what I hoped for. If he did return me, I'd have to make sure he dropped me far away from Graneden, or I'd wind up back in Lindove. Ayres had revealed there was a tracker in my head—now turned off—so what if he turned it on and I went all batty again? What if he sold me to some other warrior to compete in a different tournament that didn't require me to be a virgin? Instead of all this wondering, I should just ask the man and put myself out of my misery. But judging by his rigid back, with the deadly scythe angled across it, he didn't appear to be in a sharing mood.

He stopped suddenly and raised his arm in the air. This signal, I'd learned, meant for me to stop and keep quiet. I eased up beside him and looked around, trying in vain to hear what he did. I swore the man had the hearing and instincts of a wild animal. When he swept off his scythe and gestured for me to high-tail it into the bushes, I hurried to comply. Watching him from behind the prickly branches, I finally saw what he'd heard. A woman was approaching. She was limping, and her hair and clothes were a mess. Upon closer inspection, I recognized her as one of the contestants. The only females left now were Lissa, this woman, and me.

The woman froze when she saw Ayres. "Oh, thank God!" she gasped a moment later. Ayres remained cautious as she limped forward. She held her hands in front of her, showing she was unarmed. "Foron, my partner, was killed. Please, I have no one. I am no threat." I wanted to come out of hiding, being afraid of what Ayres might do to the poor woman, but I waited. Part of me reasoned this very well might be a trap.

"Stop," Ayres warned. His grip was tight on his weapon, and his stance was battle-ready. He suspected an attack, which made me scan the area warily for an enemy.

The woman halted and remained where she was. "These things…creatures…attacked us. Hundreds of them. We didn't stand a chance. Foron…saved me. He fought them, letting me escape. I ran. God, forgive me! I ran…and didn't look back. She dropped to her knees and sobbed.

Still, I remained in hiding. I would not move until Ayres gave me the signal. He circled the woman, and I gasped when he gave her a shove with his boot, forcing her face down onto the ground. He knelt, laying his weapon beside him, and frisked her. When he found she bore no armaments, he got to his feet and backed away, his scythe once again in his hands. "You may rise," he told her.

The woman got up and hugged herself with her arms. Her head hung low, and I could see she still shook with sobs. Ayres strode around the perimeter. Several minutes later, he finally gave me the signal to come out. I approached the pair guardedly. I could see by the grim look on Ayres' face that he wasn't pleased by our new circumstance. The woman's presence didn't thrill me either. She actually presented quite a dilemma. Ayres had stated one of the rules of the game to be no switching of partners. If your teammate was killed, you were stuck. So I didn't worry she would try to take my place. Ayres couldn't win without me. But what were we to do with her?

The woman looked at me pathetically, and I couldn't help but pity her. What if our roles were reversed? She was just a little thing, no bigger than me. Her blonde hair hung loose to her waist, a few inches longer than mine. I preferred to tame my unruly dark brown locks with a tight braid—much easier to manage. She wore the same outfit as me, her color being dark gray, though. She filled out the top half of her shirt better than I did. Her bottom was rounder and larger as well. I recalled her alien warrior had been a giant of a man with long dark hair and massive muscles. I wondered if they'd done it?

"I'm Amanda. What's your name?" I asked her.

"Jane."

Ayres glared at her. "Where were you attacked?"

Jane pointed in the direction she'd come from. "Further on down the trail. We'd just fallen asleep..." Judging from her blush, I surmised they had done it.

"We were attacked too," I told her. "But there was another warrior, and he and Ayres..."

"Enough!" Ayres grilled me with a warning glare. I guess I'd revealed too much information. He walked up the trail and signaled for me to follow him. He stopped when we were able to talk privately.

"What are you going to do?" I asked. "We can't just leave her here."

"Why not? She will have to learn to fend for herself soon enough. She will never leave this place." His face wore that cold, inhumane mask I'd seen so many times before.

My first instinct was anger. What right did these aliens have to pluck us from Earth, use us in a game, and then strand us on some wild planet? Jane, Lissa, and I were human beings, and so was that poor woman who was choked in the beginning just for rebelling. Not to mention the other women on the ship. Part of me wanted to thump Ayres in the chest or kick him in the shin. For just five minutes, I wish we could change places, and he could experience the helplessness I felt. Looking into his eyes, I could see he wouldn't understand my indignation and fury. He'd been born into a life that encouraged the subjugation of the weak. If I wanted him to see things my way, I had to use the right tactic. Hoping to stir his emotions, I got closer to him and put my hand on his chest. "Can't we keep her for a while? Just until we find someplace safe to leave her?"

"She will slow us down," he rationalized.

I moved my hand up toward the neckline of his shirt, slipping my fingers beneath while making my body flush with his. "Please? She won't be any trouble."

"No."

"Pretty please?" I stroked his chest.

Knowing well what I was doing, he smirked at me. "Do you think that is going to make me see things your way?" His hand came up and covered mine.

I shrugged and smiled up at him. "A girl can try."

Ayres looked over at Jane and then back at me again. "She can remain with us until we find somewhere safe to leave her."

That was easier than I thought. Stretching up on my tiptoes, I kissed him on the lips. "Thank you."

His face grew stern again. "But if she slows us down or causes any trouble, she will be gone."

What he meant by gone I wasn't sure. I kissed him again and then sauntered back over to Jane, Ayres right behind me. "You can stay with us. Just till we find a safe place to leave you," I told her. Though I could tell she wasn't overly thrilled with my announcement, she thanked us anyway.

The three of us continued on with Ayres leading the way and Jane and I walking side by side behind him. Jane fiddled with her hair and brushed at the dirt stains on her clothes. I remembered her from the fight ring on the ship. Her hair had been in a long braid then. She'd sucker punched a brunette and tripped a girl with short, light brown hair. I guess she'd done the best she could under the circumstances. I noticed her eyes kept fixating on Ayres's back.

"Don't worry about Ayres," I told her. "He's grouchy like that all the time."

"So was Foron," she said. "All of them seemed to have a bitch on."

I smiled. "So, what part of Earth are you from?"

"New York. Not the big city, but a little town named Cherry Creek."

"I was taken from a small town as well. I guess that's how they plan it," I said.

"My stepfather wouldn't allow me to leave our property. I could go outside—we have a dozen acres—but no further than that. He was really strict and wouldn't let me date or have any friends. I even had to be homeschooled. Life really sucked. I think he was worried about what people would say about me. My head's been really messed up the past few years. I think he thought I was going crazy."

"Your head was messed up because you were implanted with a tracking device. And your loving stepfather was most likely an alien."

Jane didn't appear surprised. "Foron told me a bunch of stuff. He mentioned the Trackers from Calixtus and the implant. I guess your Ayres told you as well."

My Ayres. I kind of liked the sound of that. "Yeah, he did. I suppose there's no need to hide stuff from us anymore."

"Doesn't it piss you off? All of this? I mean, who the hell do they think they are? That woman, the one who spoke up at the start of the game—she had it right. I should have supported her."

"So should I. And now she's dead."

Jane looked at me. "No, she's not. Foron told me she was just knocked out. That alien—I don't remember his name—had a reputation for doing that."

"What a relief. I wonder what's gonna happen to her, and all the other girls. It doesn't seem likely they'd let them go. Not after all that time invested in keeping them virgins."

"Foron said most of them are returned to Earth after the game's over, unless their alien decides to keep them. It's really up to the men. Some of the warriors can't help themselves and wind up having sex with their captive. If that happens, she can no longer be used in the game. So, she's either sent home or kept."

"That doesn't seem fair. What about what she wants? Doesn't she get a choice?"

"No. When have we ever been given a choice about any of this?" Jane said bitterly.

"The ones that are left virgins and returned to Earth, what happens to them? Are they put back in place only to be taken again for next year's tournament?"

"Possibly, if the warrior's entry is accepted again. If not, she waits until he can use her, or he may sell her to someone else. If she gets too old, or something happens and she's no longer suitable for the tournament, then they deactivate her tracker, and she can go on with her life."

"Such that it is," I said sarcastically. I thought about those poor girls who were sent back to Earth, virgins or not, telling tales about being abducted by aliens, and never to be taken seriously. Even worse would be the fate of the women who were kept against their will and taken to Calixtus. God only knew what would become of them. I stared at Ayres and wondered what my fate would be. As Jane said, it was all up to the warrior and what he wanted.

CHAPTER 13

Foron had shared a lot of information with Jane. Fat lot of good it would do her here, rotting on Taleon for the rest of her days. Looking at her, I wondered if she'd come to terms with her fate. After a harrowing experience with attacking Varlings and losing her alien, she didn't seem too upset. Not now anyway.

"How do you know that Foron didn't make it?" I asked her.

She appeared startled at my question. "No one could have survived that. Those things were everywhere at once. I'm lucky to have made it out alive."

"Yeah, lucky," I agreed. Even so, I wasn't as sure as Jane was about Foron being dead. I wouldn't count him out too soon, and I was pretty sure Ayres felt the same way. Foron's weapon had been a long battle-axe that appeared to be made entirely of steel, sporting a giant blade. It probably shot off laser beams as well. A formidable weapon against underfed, poorly armed natives, even if there were droves of them.

Ayres called a halt a while later and gave us fruit

to eat. "There is a stream," he pointed, "down there. You can drink the water. Do not wander too far." He directed this last bit at Jane. I already knew the rules.

Ayres walked over and sat down, leaning against the trunk of a tree, and began eating some purple-looking thing. Jane and I had each been handed something pink with fuzzy skin shaped like a banana. "Want to get a drink?" I asked her.

"Sure." We wandered down to the stream and sat at the water's edge. We chatted for a bit while we ate, and then I went off to relieve myself in the bushes, first making a quick check for any of those spy bubbles. When I returned, Jane was gone. I walked back up the slight hill to find her sitting with Ayres. He was smiling at something she was saying. Her hands were making big, gesturing motions as though she were telling a story.

"What's so amusing?" They both stared at me, making me feel like an intruder.

"Jane was telling me about when Foron took her from Earth."

"Oh." I remembered my capture, and nothing about it had been the least bit entertaining.

Ayres got to his feet and brushed flecks of purple off his pants. "Let's go. We'll be out of the jungle soon, and the terrain will be difficult to travel."

The jungle hadn't been much of a trial. The path had been easy to follow, though it seemed to be ever-changing. Earlier, I'd asked Ayres how he knew where we were going. He'd said the competing warriors had spent several days on board the ship reviewing visual maps so they knew what route to follow. They'd also been shown more challenging, but quicker alternative routes. This time, as we walked, Jane did her best to keep up with Ayres. She asked him several questions, which I knew would annoy him, but he appeared to be practicing restraint. Perhaps he simply preferred blondes? I hung back and watched the two of them strolling along. I grudgingly admitted they made an attractive couple.

We reached the edge of the jungle in what I'd estimated to be hours later, and I stared in amazement at the landscape beyond. Where the jungle had been green mountains and massive trees with dangling vines, the sight before us was completely alien and like nothing I'd ever seen or even imagined before. Slightly similar to the red-sand desert landscape we'd encountered upon first arrival, stretching before us was a sandy, barren landscape. The sand, however, was multicolored with flecks of it glinting like diamonds in the waning sunshine. Gentle hills with bright green, red, and yellow tufts of pointy grass pointed up towards the sky.

Jane walked beside me now, Ayres having given her the cold shoulder some time ago. She seemed as awe-struck as me over the scenery. "Wow, how unusual. Can't mistake not being on Earth now," she said.

I nodded in agreement, still feeling slightly annoyed with how she'd tried cozying up to Ayres. Her flirty behavior made me wonder if she had some plan in mind. What was to stop Ayres from winning the game with me, but asking for Jane as a boon? Of course, he had to ask for his brother's freedom, but suppose he also got to choose who left the planet with him? What would happen to me then? Hopefully, we'd find a safe place to leave Jane soon—if Ayres was still willing.

"Careful where you step," Ayres said, slowing his pace so that we all walked together. "Those plants," he pointed, "are poisonous to the touch. And just because something might look similar to what you've eaten before, don't assume it is safe. Ask me first before you touch."

Jane and I both nodded in understanding.

"I want to travel for a while longer before we rest for the night. We will need to find some shelter—it is not safe out in the open." He didn't elaborate.

"You're not going to leave me here, are you?" Jane asked, her lips pouty and her chest thrust out.

Spare me.

Ayres gazed at her with no emotion in his expression. "Not here, not yet. But soon."

Jane didn't appear happy with that announcement. She was sullen and silent as we continued trudging on. When the three moons rose high up in the sky, shining brightly, and the sky turned dark, Ayres finally settled on a place to stop. A bunch of trees with tangled limbs formed a crude circle, their branches turned in to form an overhead covering. All three of us laid down on the sand, Ayres and I side by side, and Jane a few feet away. It took me a while to fall asleep, but sometime during the night I awoke to find Ayres' arm wrapped around me. He'd pulled me closer to him, and the back of me was nestled against his front. The heat coming from his body warmed me and sent a shiver down my spine as well. With a contented sigh, I drifted off.

When I awoke, it was to the tinkle of Jane's laughter. I sat up and rubbed at my eyes before getting to my feet. I climbed out from the protection of the trees and casually strolled over to where my companions stood. Jane had her back to me, but I could see she was once again regaling Ayres with her silly stories—

ones that had her reaching out to pat his chest in mock outrage.

"You rogue warriors think you can just take any pretty girl you wish," she gushed, not sounding the least bit irritated.

Ayres met my gaze as I came up before them. "Good. You are ready?" he asked.

"Actually, I need to…ah…"

Jane's eyes flashed with amusement as she turned to stare at me. "Well, get going then. Don't dawdle."

Yeah, fuck you.

Behind the cover of the trees where we'd slept, I took a moment of privacy, all the while my teeth gnashed over the sound of Jane's bantering voice in the distance. Dropping her off somewhere no longer made me feel guilty.

We continued on our journey, trudging across the hot, glistening, multi-colored sand. Shade was practically non-existent, and finding food and water was an even rarer occurrence. My body grew weak after several hours. My braid hung damply, and my skin felt hot. The only satisfaction I had was seeing Jane just as miserable. Ayres walked first in our line, followed by Jane, with me taking up the rear. Ayres turned around several times, grilling me with his eyes, and gestured for me to keep up with him. God forbid anything happen to his sidekick. Several bubble viewers floated along with us later on our trek. At first, I thought I was seeing a mirage, but when it registered what they were, I gave one the finger and stuck my tongue out at another.

"What the hell are those things?" Jane asked.

"Ayres said they're like little cameras used to view us. Seers, he called them."

"Oh." Jane primped before one, suddenly aware she was being watched.

Ayres stopped when half a dozen more of the things showed up. "Something is happening," he said, waiting for us to catch up to him.

"What? Why do you think…"

"A—caw, a—caw!" came a scream from overhead.

All three of us froze and tilted our heads up to the sky. Jane gasped in fright. "What is it? What's that noise?" she cried.

Overhead, a sudden swarm of large bird-like creatures with wide feathered wings gathered.

"Dregers," Ayres fumed. "Bloody hell!" He swung off his scythe and took up a battle stance. "Stay close."

Jane pushed herself up against his back. Irritated,

Ayres shifted away from her. "You must make a run for it," he said to her.

"But you just said to stay close to you!" she argued.

"No. You need to run...now!" He gestured toward a cluster of high, sharp rocks about a hundred yards away. "I will draw their attention."

Jane looked unsure, but seeing the intent on Ayres' face, she finally took off at a run. Then he turned his gaze on me. I looked back at him stubbornly.

"I'm not leaving you," I warned him.

A brief smile touched his lips, and his eyes flashed. "Of course you're not." He turned his eyes back toward the fleeing Jane, and his mouth returned to a grim line. Her sudden sprint caught the attention of the Dregers, and several of them screamed out and soared after her. As they whipped past us, lowering toward the ground, I could see them more clearly.

"Oh my God! They're people. Bird people." Though their arms were covered with feathers, their heads and faces definitely resembled the Varlings I'd seen earlier—who appeared to resemble primitive Earthmen. Some of them were females; telltale breasts poked out from their chests. They wore no clothing. All of their lower regions were also feather-covered. Their hands had sharp talons for fingernails.

I watched in amazement as the rest of them, seeing their comrades race after Jane, flew after her as well. Jane, hearing the screams overhead, slowed her pace and stared upward. She cried out as two of the largest bird-men swooped down and snatched her by her arms.

"No!" I cried. I began to race toward her, but Ayres stopped me.

"Stay still," he warned.

Jane continued to struggle, but once her captors had her high up above the ground, she stopped. Her head dropped forward, and she hung completely still. Fainted, I surmised. We watched as the swarm flew off, becoming small dark specks in the sky.

I turned on Ayres, yanking free of his grip. "You set her up!"

He shrugged. "Would you rather they had taken you?"

I didn't know what to say. But as he turned away and resumed walking across the barren land, his weapon still in his hands, I realized something about my companion.

He could be a cold-hearted son-of-a-bitch when he needed to be.

CHAPTER 14

The problem of finding a safe place to ditch Jane was no longer an issue. Part of me, I must admit, felt a little relieved when those bird-men flew off with her. A bigger part of me felt guilty for feeling that way. At least I didn't have to contend with her flirty laugh anymore. Also, there'd be no more worrying if Ayres would decide he liked her better and leave me to rot in this place.

I eyed Ayres critically as he and I sat by a small fire surrounded by tall trees. The forest we'd entered a couple of hours ago—I estimated—seemed so much like one in Graneden that it made me feel homesick. The night sky was lit up with zillions of twinkling stars, and the rustling of small animals all around reminded me of the nights I'd spent with Uncle Mick at the cottage. I refused to even think about alien Aunt Erin—the traitor.

Ayres had caught some kind of large rodent and roasted it over the fire on a stick. The smell of it cooking made my mouth drool. Disgusting, but I was starving for something substantial to eat.

"Those things that took Jane, the Dregers, we don't have creatures like that on Earth," I said.

"I know."

Of course he did. "What'll they do with her?" Please don't say they'll eat her.

"Depends. From what I know, they will probably breed with her. I have heard they prefer to capture alien females because their own have trouble giving birth."

A vision of those sharp talons flashed in my mind. "Will she be okay, do you think?"

He stared into my eyes. "A worse fate could have befallen her here. She is better off with the Dregers."

"You mean there are worse things?"

"Far worse. We have been lucky not meet up with giant wild beasts or smaller, but more ferocious tribes."

"More ferocious than the Varlings?" I didn't even want to consider the giant wild beasts.

"Far worse," he repeated.

"Do you think the other competitors have gotten far?" Lissa's Oro was a tough alien. Hopefully, they were still in the game.

"Two are out so far. That only leaves one against us."

I hoped our paths wouldn't cross. Ayres and

Oro were both huge and strong. I wouldn't want to see them battle each other. The thought of Oro coming for me made me shiver.

Ayres reached out his hand to me. "Are you cold? Come sit by me." I shimmied over and curled up against his side. He gripped the stick again, needing both hands to slowly turn the cooking meat. "After we eat, we'll sleep."

"Oh." I'd been hoping, now that we were alone, he'd want to love me again. It'd been a while. Well, only a couple of days, but still…

We ate the rodent and then lay out side by side. The warm glow of the fire made dancing shadows against the trees. I reached for Ayres' hand and took it in mine. The strength and firmness I felt made me antsy for some attention. His eyes were closed, but as I rolled to my side and put my hand on his crotch, they opened. He allowed me to stroke him to hardness through his clothing before he sat up and pulled off his shirt. When he looked at me, I was pulling mine off as well.

"Anxious?" he asked, his lips curled into a sarcastic grin.

"Don't you want to?" Maybe he was too tired? Or he could be thinking about Jane?

He looked down at the outline of his hard cock

straining against his pants. "What do you think?"

"That looks uncomfortable," I said innocently. "You should take them off."

"As you wish." He got to his feet and lowered his pants; his cock sprang free. When he would have sat down again, I scooted over and took hold of his prick in my hand, stopping him in his tracks. In Lindove, I'd heard the older women talk about having a man in their mouths. I'd already acted out this scenario with Ayres dozens of times in my horny Episodes, so the reality should be a piece of cake.

Gently, my tongue flicked out to lick his tip. When he groaned, I took it as a good sign. Growing bolder, I swirled my tongue around his rim and sucked the head of his cock into my mouth. Deep I took him, as far as I could without choking, praying all the while I wasn't making a fool of myself. By the movement of his hips and the growling noises he made, I figured I was doing okay. When he could stand it no more, he gently pushed me back and lowered me to the ground. He made a grab for my ankles, and after yanking off my boots, he pulled off my pants in one swift movement and tossed them aside. Then he was opening my thighs wide apart with his hands as he settled between them.

I felt the head of his cock push against me, causing me to lift my bottom and welcome him. He plunged deep inside me with one thrust, as he had the first time he'd taken me. But this time, he didn't wait for me to grow accustomed to his size. Seeing as I was no longer a virgin, I guess he didn't feel the need to go slow. He began to pump right away, causing me to cry out in delight. This was the man he really was—the warrior, the man who would take without mercy.

He continued to thrust inside of me for a long while. Quickly at first, only to slow his pace just as he sensed I was about to come. My body twitched in agitation. No matter what I did, be it squeezing my thighs or my passage, he soldiered on. I arched my body and scratched his back, all to no avail. The look on his face was one of pure concentration. Perhaps he wasn't as immune to my charms as he pretended? I couldn't stand it anymore. He'd brought me to the brink several times, only to tease me with the promise of fulfillment.

"Damn it, Ayres!" He reached down to squeeze my boob, ignoring my plea. I was a mass of horny hysteria before he finally took mercy on me. He sank deep inside me with a mighty thrust and stilled his movements. Sensing he was near completion, I squeezed tight and took my pleasure, crashing into wave after wave of ecstasy. It was several moments before I realized he'd gone at the same time as me.

"You're an asshole." He rolled off of me, and I snuggled against his side. Though I didn't look at his face, I could practically feel his superior grin. He may have made me writhe and beg this time, but next time, I determined, I'd be the one who would make him squirm.

We awoke to the sound of chirping birds, and it surprised me to find Ayres still on his back beside me. Usually, I awoke last, and he had to urge me to get up and get moving. His eyes shot open suddenly, probably feeling my lingering gaze. He sat up and ran a hand over his shorn head.

"So, what's on the agenda for today?" I gave him what I believed to be a sexy smile, hoping he might forgo our journey for an hour or so.

No such luck. He got to his feet, and I watched his backside in regret while he donned his clothing. I got up and dressed as well. "We are over halfway. The next trek will be difficult."

"More difficult than the scorching desert?"

Seeing my glum look, Ayres reached out and brushed a stray hair from my face. Such a tender gesture for a deadly man. "Where we go next will be mountainous and very cold. I will have to hunt for furs to protect us from freezing to death."

From boiling to freezing. This trip just gets

better all the time. "Hunt what? Those giant beasts you spoke of?" I didn't like the idea of that. But I disliked the idea of freezing even more. "Isn't it dangerous?" I asked when he nodded.

"There were several tracks on the trail. The Daeodon, I believe. Should be large enough to provide a warm fur for each of us."

"What is it?"

"The Daeodon is actually an ancient relative of Earth's wild boar. It lived in North America and went extinct about 18 million years ago, or so I was told. We named Taleon's beast as such because of its striking similarity."

Modern-day boars on Earth were deadly animals. Huge and powerful with those dangerous tusks, able to gore a man or other animal in seconds. I couldn't imagine what an ancient relative of it would look like. Probably even bigger and meaner, as most of the ancestors of Earth's animals were.

"So do we just carry on until we spot one?"

"I was hoping we'd come across one last night. The fire must have kept it away. They usually hunt at dusk, so tonight we'll set a trap."

"With what?"

"I'll snare a couple of sways—the furry creature we ate last night. It has to work, or we won't keep to our time frame. We must reach the cold land by mid-morning tomorrow. But without furs for protection…"

"We'll freeze to death."

He nodded. "We can bring the meat along as well, as there'll be nothing to eat."

We followed the trail through the forest, stopping along the way at streams to refresh ourselves and picking weird berries to eat. Ayres allowed me to strip naked and splash around in the water for a few minutes, which was a delightful treat. I had hoped he would join me, but always the warrior, he stood guard and only rinsed off his face and neck. When the sun began its descent, Ayres hunted a couple of sways and lay them down as bait in a clearing where he'd ambush his prey. He made me scale a tree while he took to hiding behind a thicket to wait. Soon enough, we heard the telltale rustling and snorting of something large coming our way. From my high perch—over Ayres' hiding spot and to his left—I spotted it first.

"Shit," I whispered. It did indeed resemble a huge boar. Its thick furry head was about three feet long, and it must have been about six feet high at the shoulder. Its body was covered with brown and black spiky fur. When it lifted its head to sniff the air, I noticed it didn't have any tusks, but its mouth was shaped like a huge dog's, sporting giant, razor-sharp teeth. It was bigger than a polar bear. I watched Ayres swing off his scythe and position himself to move. Was he actually going to take that thing on?

The boar moved cautiously toward the sways, no doubt smelling our scent as well. The animal turned around in a circle a couple of times and then slowly moved in to snuffle at the ground by the bait. Satisfied, it began to eat. The snap and crunch of bones drifted up to my ears. My gaze flashed to Ayres, who was ready to spring. Everything seemed to move in slow motion in that moment.

Ayres jumped out, and the beast swung round to face him. They both stayed frozen in place, sizing each other up. The beast was the first to move. It growled, displaying all of its teeth, and bowed its head as though to charge. Ayres stood, feet braced wide apart, arms out in front of him, holding his scythe at an angle. When the Daeodon lunged, he was ready. They came together in a clash. Ayres held his ground at first, but moments later, he went down.

"Ayres!" I screamed, scrambling down from the tree. I paused on a lower branch to see what was happening. All I could see was the great beast lying atop Ayres, and one booted foot beneath the heap of fur and muscle. "Get off him!"

Further down, I climbed and finally jumped

to the ground, causing the animal's head to dart in my direction. Bent forward, keeping my arms wide to make myself appear larger, I walked toward the pair slowly. The beast shifted as I changed direction, circling behind them. The movement caused its body to lift slightly, giving Ayres a chance to slip out. It was all he needed. Suddenly, he was rolling away, weapon in hand, and while still in a crouched position, swung his weapon in an arc, making contact with the animal's leg. The beast howled in rage and swung back to Ayres. Ayres got to his feet, and I saw with relief that he appeared unharmed.

"Come for me," he taunted, not taking his eyes from his opponent.

But then, another sound from behind the pair caught my attention. A great crashing noise coming closer and closer soon revealed, to my horror, another beast approaching.

CHAPTER 15

"Ayres! Behind you..." My cry got his attention. Instead of turning, he charged forward and sliced at the first beast with lightning-fast blows, drawing blood and anguished screams. Once the animal lay at his feet, he spun round and faced his next opponent, who stood only yards away, head ducked and pawing at the ground. This Daeodon, at least, was slightly smaller than the first. Probably a female, I surmised.

Ayres, despite the terrible battle, barely seemed to be breaking a sweat. I marveled at his strength and stamina. I myself would have been a quivering mass of tears, rocking back and forth by now.

The animal looked past Ayres toward me and then to its fallen mate, lying in a bloodied heap on the ground. It threw back its head and let loose a heart-wrenching cry.

"Move on," Ayres urged her. "There's been enough killing today." His voice was gentle, and I'm sure I detected a hint of regret.

The great beast shook its mighty head, snorted a few times, and then, to my amazement, turned and crashed away through the trees. Ayres watched it flee for several moments before he turned back toward his kill. His gaze flashed to me, and the line of his mouth drew even grimmer.

"You should not have moved," he said.

I didn't come toward him. I took a step back instead. "I was afraid for you."

He stalked slowly forward, going around the carcass, and came to a stop right in front of me. I had to tilt my head back to look into his eyes. They were cold. He reached out a hand and grabbed hold of the back of my braided hair, wrenching it tight. "Do not defy me again. All of this will have been for nothing if you foolishly disregard my warnings." He gave me a bit of a shake and then pushed me from him, causing me to stumble. I steadied myself and watched him turn his back on me.

"Fuck you!"

He stopped and turned slowly back around. "What did you say to me, girl?"

Though I trembled in fear, I held my ground. "If I hadn't distracted the beast, you would probably still be lying beneath it. You should be thanking me, asshole."

Stalking forward, he stopped before me once more and raised his hand as though to strike. I flinched, but remained still, facing him in defiance. He scared me, and yet, I knew he wouldn't hurt me. Not much anyway. He needed me alive for the game.

As though reading my mind, he lowered his hand. "I may need you now, but once the tournament is over, be assured I will punish you."

"For what? Speaking my mind? Can't your tiny ego get over the fact that I helped save your ass?" Damn my big mouth!

His hand flashed out and grabbed hold of my throat, just as that other giant had done to his woman when we arrived. His grip was tight, but not choking. "Remember that you rely on my goodwill for your survival."

"As you rely on my survival for your brother's freedom," I reminded him.

"That may be so. You had best pray to your god that we win. If we lose, I'll have no further use of you. Except perhaps to cater to my baser needs," he said with a sneer.

Had I actually thought I was falling for this guy? Of all the arrogant, egotistical, self-serving jackasses I'd ever known or met, or seen on TV, he was by far the worst. "When we win, I expect you to keep up your end of the bargain. Freedom, and return to Earth, me and my friends. I have no use for you either." A stupid, cursed tear slipped down my cheek.

Ayres let go of me and strode away, without another word, toward the Deaodon. He used his weapon to begin skinning it for its fur. Seeing the cold fury of my companion, I had a feeling I was gonna need that fur.

Ayres hadn't bothered to touch me when we lay down to sleep that night. He'd hung the furs he'd cut over branches and used some of the hide to wrap thick chunks of meat for us to cook along our frozen journey. By mid-morning, just as Ayres predicted, we entered into a snowy land and began the slow climb upward into the mountain. The higher we got, the more snow-covered and colder it became. We'd barely spoken a word to each other. I had no desire to say anything to him anyway. What a pompous ass, I thought, glaring daggers at his back.

The ever-present viewer bubbles floated around us. They'd been there yesterday when Ayres fought the beast. I suppose I should have noticed by the number of them that something big was going on. Ayres had probably noticed them as well. Maybe that's why he figured he didn't need my warning about another beast, or my distraction to free him from the first one. The bubbles didn't interfere, however, with anything we did. And if he thought a bunch of them would distract a Deaodon lying atop him, he was a fool as well as an ass.

We climbed higher. The path we took was an easy incline, so I wasn't overtaxed. The snow was becoming a problem. Wind was stronger than it'd been below, and with it, the heavy falling flakes obscured my view. Ayres walked ahead of me, but now I could barely see him. He slowed once in a while to allow me to catch up, but I could tell he was irritated at having to wait. He paused at the top of a turn ahead, and once I was beside him, he reached to pull the fur I clutched around my shoulders tighter. It was heavy and awkward to hold onto, the snow weighing it down even more. Thankfully, Ayres had the meat sacks slung over his shoulder, so I didn't have that burden to bear.

"There are caves ahead. We'll shelter there for the night and have a fire and something to eat," he said, speaking over my head.

"Good." We hadn't eaten all day, and I felt lightheaded.

We drudged onward for a long while before Ayres finally led us alongside a rocky area of the mountain. Once I was close enough, I could see there was a low opening. He crouched and entered the mouth of the cave, with me following close behind. Once inside, we could both stand up. I was surprised to see his scythe light up in the darkness like a torch. Ayres went to the center of the interior, where a circle of rocks sat ready for a fire. How convenient. Since we were on the main trail, it made sense that this cave would probably be one of many to have been used in the past by other contestants. Ayres tossed his fur over to the back wall and pulled off his scythe. He stuck it into the hard dirt floor so it stood upright like a lamp. From his pocket, he produced an instrument to make fire. There wasn't much wood in the fire pit, but I could see there was more against another wall. The cave was a good size. About twenty feet deep, fifteen feet wide, and I would guess about forty feet high—some parts appeared to go much higher than that.

I shivered, wrapped up in my fur, while he got the fire going. Seeing as he wasn't using it, I took a seat on his discarded fur and watched as he found a thin stick and speared a piece of meat onto it. He angled it over the fire, sticking one end in the dirt, and used other sticks to hold it up so it sat just over the flames. Then he went and grabbed more wood for the fire. All the while I sat there like a useless dolt. The silence was only interrupted by the sizzling of the fat from the meat as it dripped off into the flames. Exhausted and mesmerized by the glow of the fire, I lay down and drifted off to sleep. I awoke later when I felt Ayres' booted foot tapping me on the ass.

"Time to eat," he said.

I rubbed at my eyes and lumbered over to the fireside where he now sat. He handed me a piece of meat, and I began to eat. There was a wooden bowl beside the fire that held water, probably melted snow. Ayres ate and then drank some of the water before passing it to me. I drank some and handed it back to him.

"That was good. Thanks," I said.

He grunted in response.

"So, is this how it's gonna be between us now?" I demanded. "Look, I'm sorry I didn't follow your orders, captain, but I thought we were a team. You know, helping each other? I don't know what things are like on Calixtus, but on Earth, women are quite capable of handling things. We're not all helpless little powder puffs."

"Some of those women you speak of are taken for games on my planet. I'm well aware that many female Earthlings are quite capable."

"But you don't put me in that category?" Hauled before their panel, I'd been called helpless and pathetic.

"If you were, you would not be here," he informed me.

"Ah, yes. You need weak, crazy girls for your manly men to protect."

"The implant caused the confusion," he reminded me.

"So just weak then? Is that really the type of woman you like?" He seemed to like me just fine when he was fucking my brains out.

He shrugged.

"Well, I may not be big and strong, but I do have a brain in my head. I can help you if you'll just get over yourself."

"We leave at first light. You'd best get some rest," he said.

How infuriating he was! He didn't even consider me worthy enough to argue with. Once this stupid tournament was over, I hoped I never saw him again. I got to my feet and started toward the exit.

"Where are you going?" he demanded.

"I have to pee. I think I'm capable of doing at least that without your help or guidance," I snapped.

Several feet later and a few turns around the rocky area, I found a place for privacy. Once finished, I brushed the snow off myself as I walked slowly back toward the cave. Viewer bubbles floated around. Since I only spotted two of them, I wasn't concerned. But as I rounded the next corner, just before the cave, a flicker of multi-colored waves of light caught my attention.

"What the hell?"

Suddenly, right in front of me, a holographic image of the leader Baynar appeared. He stared at me with a patronizing leer.

"Well done, Amanda," he said. "Be proud, you have come far."

"Ah, thanks," I said. At least he was impressed with me.

"Before you head back to Ayres, I want to speak with you alone."

"Okay."

"I have a deal to offer you," he said.

"What kind of deal?" He gave me the creeps.

"I can arrange to get you out of there right now. You never wanted any part of this anyway. I can have you and your friends returned to Earth. All you have to do is say the word."

"I can go home? Leave…just like that? What about the tournament and Ayres?"

He shrugged. "You don't owe him anything. Look at what he's done to you: implanting a device that made you appear insane; killed your family; took you from Earth against your will; subjected you to a life and death game. And all for what? To free his criminal brother? He's used you, Amanda."

Most of what Baynar said was true. Yet, he was a part of it. It was how things were done on his planet. They'd been using Earth and humans for thousands of years for entertainment. No way did I buy that he was all of a sudden developing a conscience. "In the first place, Aunt Erin wasn't my family," I informed him.

"But Ayres killed your uncle," Baynar said.

"No. That woman killed him. Ayres told me," I insisted.

"Oh, Ayres told you that, did he?" he chuckled a little, like I was an idiot.

"And second, how did you know what Ayres would ask as his boon? I thought it was private till the end."

"His brother is set for execution. It's obvious he'll ask for his freedom." He waved his hands around as though to dismiss my objections. "None of this concerns you. Ayres' problems are his own. You can be free, now. All you have to do is accept my help."

Tempting as it sounded, I was no fool. I didn't trust this guy. Something about him made my skin crawl. What was up with his last-ditch offer? This tournament was rigged. He would leave Ayres here to rot and execute his brother without a second thought. But since Baynar had approached me, I was worried. If I declined his offer, what would stop him from removing me from the game? He obviously wanted me out of the way.

"Thank you for the offer," I said carefully. "But can I think about it?"

"What is there to think about?" he snapped. "I'm offering you freedom, foolish girl."

"Oh, my God! Look at that!" I cried, pointing over Baynar's holographic shoulder.

"What? What is it?" Baynar swung round, but of course, he couldn't see anything.

"Avalanche!" I yelled and took off full speed toward the mouth of the cave.

CHAPTER 16

Ayres stormed out of the cave just as I dived in. We bonked heads, causing me to bounce back into the snow, crying out in pain. He pulled me inside, then rushed out to look around.

"I heard you yell avalanche," he said, coming back in. "Nothing's going on out there."

I looked at him grimly and rubbed my head. "There's a lot more going on out there than you know."

He crossed his arms and glared at me. "Don't play games with me, Amanda. I know you're angry, but that's no reason to start..."

"I'm not making things up," I interrupted. "You have to listen to me, Ayres. The game...it's rigged!" He recoiled as though I'd struck him. Before he could recover, I went on. "Your leader—that Baynar guy on board the ship—he appeared to me as a hologram. He waited till I was alone. We're close to winning, and he knows you're going to ask to have your brother freed. He offered me a deal. A deal that would free me and my friends and send us back to Earth, and leave you here to rot. The game is rigged, I swear it."

Ayres said nothing.

"Baynar told me you killed Uncle Mick and that I don't owe you anything. He's trying to turn me against you. I was afraid of what he'd do to me if I refused his deal. He's exposed himself to me. I'm a dead girl walking. I didn't know what to do, so I yelled 'avalanche' and ran."

Ayres walked over to his fur and sat down, putting his head into his hands. It worried me, seeing him like this. He appeared in shock and utterly defeated. I tiptoed over and sat down beside him.

"Are you all right? You believe me, don't you?"

He lifted his head and stared into my eyes. "Yes, I believe you, Amanda. You have no reason to lie to me."

When he continued to stare at me, I flushed. "What?"

"Why didn't you take his deal? He's right, you don't owe me anything."

I shivered, recalling Baynar's cold stare. "I don't trust him. How could I trust someone who's willing to cheat like that? Besides, I couldn't just leave you here. Your brother is counting on you."

He smiled at me.

"And it's not like I have anything to rush back to anyhow, except a straitjacket and rubber room that is. We're gonna win this tournament, Ayres. You and me. Together." Don't ask me why I was suddenly team Ayres, especially after how he'd treated me. But the thought of his own kind turning on him made me suddenly protective.

Ayres pulled me into his arms and kissed the top of my head. It was strangely endearing. "I was afraid something like this would happen," he said.

I stiffened and pulled away. "What do you mean? You thought the game was fixed?"

"There's been some underhanded dealing going on on Calixtus. Warriors talk. Apparently, a lot of money has changed hands. I suppose Baynar and his people bet on the wrong man."

"So what do we do? It's obvious they're going to do everything they can to make sure we don't win." Including killing me.

"There's no way Baynar and his cohorts can allow you to live now that you know the truth," Ayres said, confirming my fears. "We'll have to outsmart them."

"How?" Our every move was watched. They probably knew what we were going to do even before we did it. Plus, they may be helping the other team. Lissa and Oro were probably the favorites to win. Good for Lissa—at least she may survive this ordeal—

but bad for us.

"We resort to plan B."

"I didn't know you had a plan B," I said.

He smiled wickedly. "I'm always prepared."

When he leaned down and started kissing my neck, I found I couldn't relax. "What if they come in here now, ray guns blazing?"

"They won't," he assured me. "They'll rig some sort of accident along the way. The world will want to be watching when we meet our demise. Better for ratings, and it'll appear to have happened spontaneously."

"Oh." I leaned my head against him, enjoying the hard muscle beneath my cheek. If this was our last night together, I wanted to enjoy it. I closed my eyes and tried to tune out my fears. Ayres's hands worked their way under my shirt, and I felt the cool air on my belly as he lifted it. "I'm cold."

He stood up and stripped off all his clothes, then began pulling at mine. If this was his idea of warming me up, he was failing. I curled into a shivering ball until he sat beside me and pulled me into his arms. Warm kisses rained on my face, and warm hands stole all over my body—stroking here, caressing there. Gradually, my body responded and soon stopped shivering. My breath came out in little pants as Ayres' hand slipped between my thighs. The first time we'd done it had been slow and gentle. The second, frantic and forceful. What would the third time be like? A combination of both seemed ideal.

He laid me back and leaned over to lick and kiss my breasts. He suckled my nipples, one, then the other, making them both stand at attention. All the while, his hand stroked between my legs. I spread my thighs wide and was rewarded for my compliance with a large finger slipped into my passage. Now he licked a trail from my breasts down to my belly. A second finger slipped inside of me. His movements were slow, drawn out. It would take him forever to put out the fire raging inside of me.

"Ayres," I cried. Damn him, he was taunting me on purpose. I wanted him inside of me…now. Suddenly, I felt like such a harlot, but I didn't care. If my life were to end tomorrow, I wanted to die with an ache in my crotch and a smile on my face. I almost forgot my resolve to torment him this time around.

"Yes?" he practically purred.

"Fuck me already."

"Such language, Amanda. I'm shocked."

Wiggling around until I got free of him, I pushed at his chest, urging him to lie on his back. Torment me, will you? I got down to business with his cock, licking the long length of him until I had him gripping the furs. Next, I slipped him into my mouth and deep-throated as far as I could go, all the while cuddling his ball sack with both hands. Now, who wants it bad? For several minutes, I sucked and teased until he broke out in a sheen of sweat. At last, taking mercy on him, I straddled his body and guided his enormous cock to my opening. I slowly sat up, letting him slide inside— controlling the speed at which he advanced. He gripped my hips, and I began to ride him like a cowgirl.

"Hang on," he ground out.

My hands braced against his chest until I let go and brazenly gripped my breasts, lifting and squeezing them as though an offering. The effect seemed to turn him on even more. Swiftly, he rolled me over onto my back. Now he was the one on top and in control.

"You want me to fuck you?" he demanded.

"Yes!"

His cock pushed inside of me right to the hilt. He thrust over and over until I was in a mindless frenzy. Soon, my world exploded, and for the first time, I screamed my head off. I don't know what came over me in that instant, be it the frantic sex or the threat of death, but my guard slipped. "I love you," I cried.

Ayres didn't respond. He only increased his pace until he came as well, this time, he actually yelled.

Afterward, curled in his arms, just as I began to doze, I could have sworn I heard him whisper, "Love you, too."

But it was probably a dream.

CHAPTER 17

We got an early start the next morning. The air was freezing, but the snow had lightened up. I'd slept restlessly, being worried about what today would bring. The surrounding snowy mountains suddenly seemed much more ominous. I hoped my yelling 'avalanche' hadn't given Baynar any ideas.

Ayres was ever watchful, appearing even more so today. He wouldn't allow me to trail him by more than a few paces. When one of the viewer bubbles floated past, I was tempted to tell the world about Baynar's offer last night. How would the inhabitants of Calixtus feel knowing their precious game was rigged? When I'd made this suggestion to Ayres, he had shrugged it off.

"Won't do any good," he'd said. "No one would believe you. Besides, who's to say the viewers aren't already getting an edited version of what's happening here?"

He was right. There was no way of knowing.

"How long till we're out of the Cold Land?" I asked, shivering under my fur.

"If we keep up this pace, it should be by sundown."

Hours later, we sat by a small fire and cooked more of the Deaodon meat. We ate quickly, leery of an ambush, and continued on our way. It seemed strange that we'd been allowed to come so far. I wondered if perhaps Baynar had another fate in store for us. This was day six. Tonight, we'd reach the edge of the Safe Zone, and soon the game would be over. Had it already been almost a week? How time flew when you were playing for your life.

Sun peeked over the mountain, reflecting off the snow. My feet were freezing despite my boots, which were made more for warmer weather hiking. I had given up on feeling my hands, which gripped the edges of the fur around my shaking body. Gradually, the farther we traveled, the warmer the air became, and tufts of grass poked up through the snow. The closer we got to the Safe Zone, the more my anxiety grew. Every whisper of wind, snap of an overhead branch, or scurry in the snow made my hair stand on end.

Despite all my concerns, I was glad the end was coming—one way or another. All this stress was killing me. If by some miracle we were able to complete the game and actually win, Ayres would have his boon, and I'd be free. Back to Earth I'd go. Perhaps I'd get them to beam me somewhere safe where nobody knew who I was. I'd always wanted to see England. Maybe I could get Ayres to toss in some money as well. I deserved some compensation for all my troubles. Returning to Earth, and what would happen to me afterward, hadn't entered much into my thoughts. Ayres had been such an overwhelming presence in my life. I didn't know what I'd do once he was gone.

Gone.

A pang gripped my belly at the thought. For years, he'd tormented me; lovingly, teasingly, and terrifyingly. He'd been my constant companion for so long, I wasn't sure how to function without him. I put a hand to my head, thinking about the implant he'd hidden there to keep tabs on me. Would it remain? Could he use it to find me again…if he even wanted to? Or would he forget me easily and slide back into his life, glad to have all this trouble behind him? Welcome heat flushed over me when I remembered the feel of his hands on my body. Each touch of his lips on mine made me quiver in anticipation. And when we joined as one, I felt truly complete. Love, or lust, the reality of him was far better than any fantasy I'd had.

Ayres froze suddenly and I walked into his back. "What the h—" Rudely, I broke from my rumination.

"Shhh!" he hissed.

"Why, what's wrong?" I whispered, staring all around, expecting the worst. As usual, his supersonic hearing picked up sounds long before I did. Ayres swung off his scythe and gestured at me to take cover behind an outcropping of rock. We'd traveled for hours, and now that the sun was setting, the snowy landscape had slowly tapered off into a wave of green fields. Once I was hidden, I heard the frantic prodding steps coming from behind us.

A figure emerged, snow-covered and small. Black curls poked out from the layer of white on her head. Lissa! She ran so blindly that she almost ran into Ayres, as I had. His hand came up before she made contact and sent her reeling onto her backside. She sat there stunned, but then scrambled to get up. Ayres angled his scythe at her.

"Do not," he said.

Being a lone female, probably unarmed, I didn't think Ayres would harm her. He'd been nice enough to what's her name. I scanned the area for Oro, yet saw nothing. Surprising, considering they were the couple voted most likely to succeed. A tinge of hope entered my breast. If Oro was dead, or even wounded, and could not complete the game, Baynar would have no choice but to let us win.

I waited until Ayres gave the 'all-clear' before

I came out. When I would have bent down to Lissa, Ayres kept me at his side.

"Lissa, what's wrong? You look terrified," I said. "Where's Oro?"

"Yes, where is he?" Ayres asked coldly.

"G…gone."

"What do you mean, gone?" I asked, trying to keep the glee from my voice.

"There was…an accident. In the mountains," Lissa said, her voice choked with sobs. Maybe Baynar hijacked the wrong couple? Wouldn't he be pissed!

"What should we do?" I asked Ayres. Lissa was helpless and broken. She'd probably finally figured out she wasn't in La La Land. We couldn't just leave her here. Ayres looked out across the field. It was smooth as a golf course. Off in the distance, just visible in the dusky landscape, was a large green hill. Halfway up appeared to be a sandy area, or maybe the grass was just dead, but in the center of that was a tall white flagpole. The finish line, I supposed. We were so close…

Lissa's sobbing had no effect on Ayres. He stood stone cold, his gaze alternating from her to the white flag pole. "We can't leave her," I said.

"We will soon have no choice."

I knew he meant when the game was over. I wondered if it was possible for me to ask to have her returned to Earth along with Danny and Jack? Although the rules of the game must be followed—at least in our case—losers had to remain. All of this was so unfair. We hadn't asked for any of this, and yet, for the sake of a stupid game, our lives were irrevocably changed. I guess my miserable face made Ayres soften a bit.

"She may continue on with us for a while," he said.

I reached out to pull Lissa to her feet. "Come with us."

Her shoulders slumped, but she allowed me to guide her along, trailing Ayres as he took up the lead. We'd traveled far, and I was exhausted. I could see that Lissa was in no condition to keep going either.

"As soon as I find a suitable place, we'll rest for the night," Ayres said. There wasn't much need to hurry now, considering we were the only team remaining. Whether Baynar liked it or not, he'd have to declare us the victors tomorrow.

We had a small fire later, nestled in the center of a group of tall trees we'd hiked to, just off to the left of our destination. Ayres and I spoke softly, not wanting to disturb Lissa, who'd eaten a little of the meat offered her before she lay down to sleep. It was full dark now, and off in the dense forest beside us, I could hear strange animal sounds and rustling in the undergrowth.

So this would be our last night together. As much as I wanted to spend it making love with Ayres, I could see he was in no mood. All his attention seemed riveted on winning the game and getting his brother freed.

"What will you do now?" I asked. "Once Kenix is released, I mean."

"Get on with our lives," he said.

"Aren't you worried about Baynar? He'll know I told you about the game being rigged. Do you think he'll come after you?"

The glint in Ayres' eyes made me shiver. "He can try."

"It's not much of a life, always having to look over your shoulder. He didn't sound thrilled about you asking for your brother's freedom."

"Kenix and Baynar were never friends. My brother can be a difficult sort to abide. He is always looking for the easy way of things; never wanting to put in the time or effort."

"Is he a warrior like you?"

"A warrior, yes. Like me, no."

"You must be close for you to go through all this for him," I said.

"He is my family," he said simply.

Ayres removed his scythe and laid it beside him as he settled his back against a tree. Wanting to be close to him, I curled up between his legs and rested my head on his thigh. He'd spread my fur beneath us and generously given his to Lissa for her comfort. The soft breeze was mild, and the temperature was warm—what a difference from the cold mountains. This planet was strange, going from one extreme to another in such close range. I must have drifted off because the next thing I knew, Ayres was shifting around, and the sun was beating down on my face.

Lissa sat staring into the cold embers of the fire, her arms wrapped around her legs. She had a sad but determined look on her face. I wandered past her, saying "good morning", on my way to find a spot for privacy. She returned my greeting and then turned to continue staring at the fire pit. As I returned, Ayres was rolling up our fur and packing it into the makeshift sack he'd fashioned from part of the Deaodon's leather hide. I presumed he was packing it up to give to Lissa for her use after we were gone. Once we started out, I would broach the subject of the possibility of Lissa returning to Earth with me. It was a slim-to-none chance, but I still had to try. Lissa saw us getting ready to leave, and she got to her feet.

"What should I do with this?" She gestured to the fur at her feet.

"I have one here for you. It should be enough," Ayres told her.

"You mean when you leave me behind?" she asked. Ayres may have taken offense if her tone had been sarcastic or scornful, but it wasn't. As it was, he ignored her.

We began to make our way through the trees and head toward the wide-open field. Ayres walked first, Lissa second, while I trailed behind, trying to come up with a plan. My attention focused on finding the right words to convince Ayres that he had to ask for Lissa to be allowed to return to Earth with me. I was so deep in thought that when I saw a flash of light reflect on the trail, it didn't faze me. Probably Ayres' scythe, I figured. It'd been glinting into my eyes on and off for days now. When it flashed again, this time in my face, I lifted my gaze to frown at his back. If he didn't insist on taking the damn lead all the time…

I froze.

Ayres strolled on ahead as I'd expected, but Lissa was now right behind him. In her hands, she held a large, thin blade. She had it raised and ready to strike. "Don't!" I screamed at the same moment she stabbed the glinting steel into his back. Lissa turned and smiled at me triumphantly before she took off into the forest.

"Ayres! Ayres, no!" I ran to him as fast as I could and came around in front of him. He wore a look of shock on his face, which was rapidly turning white. He dropped to his knees, his hands now reaching to claw at his back. He grabbed hold of his scythe and swung it off to the ground. His hands stopped grappling and reached out, grabbing hold of me like a lifeline. I went down on my knees as well, holding him tight. I didn't know what to do. If I pulled out the blade, it could do more harm than good. But if I left it in…

"Ayres, please…" I couldn't stop the tears from falling.

He leaned against me, heavily now. "You…take my scythe. Protect…yourself."

"No! You stay with me. Don't you leave me." Don't you dare.

"I…I'm sorry. I…" His voice was barely a whisper. He fell forward, and I eased him to the ground. The cursed blade lay deep in his back, a stain of blood seeping around it.

That fucking bitch! Back stabbing, lying, deceitful, hateful witch!

Ayres didn't move. His breath was shallow, his lungs laboring with effort to keep him alive. We were done for. So close to the end, and yet so far. All this time, we'd been waiting for Baynar to make his move. Meanwhile, he hadn't needed to do anything—except turn my friend against me. I had no doubt he'd put her up to this.

Terrible sorrow engulfed me, along with flashes of moments Ayres and I had spent together. All of it. All the moments, the good, the bad, the ugly, and what could have been between us, whether we won the game or not. A secret part of me had sometimes hoped we would lose and have to face the rest of our lives on this cursed planet—because we'd be together. I'd daydreamed of us winning, of Ayres returning me to Earth, only to come storming back into my life, declaring he couldn't live without me.

How would I live without him?

Rage pushed my sorrow aside. It crept up my body like a slow-moving tide until it overcame me, heating me up till I felt I would boil with it. Along with it came crystal clarity as to what I would do next.

Without another thought, I picked up Ayres' scythe, struggling a moment over the weight of it. Rage making me strong, I gripped the weapon firmly and strode off to the green valley.

CHAPTER 18

The couple before me crossed the field in the direction of the hill. They weren't rushing. There was no need, now that the dirty deed had been done. Oro appeared healthy and hale, not lying dead or dying somewhere as Lissa had made him out to be. He walked ahead of her, just as Ayres had always insisted on doing with me. Lissa lagged behind, probably in shock or awe over her actions. I took a deep breath, gathered my strength, and began to run.

The soft grass beneath my feet covered the sound of my approach. Before they could turn and react, I was upon them, Lissa being the first to see me. Whether she'd finally heard my ragged breath or felt some tingle of danger, she suddenly turned and froze. As she let loose a scream, I raised Ayres scythe using all my strength and brought it down. I smacked her in the side of the head with the flat of the blade. Not a deathblow, but damaging all the same. She fell like a stone to the ground.

Now I had Oro's attention.

He let loose a battle cry that in other

circumstances might have turned my knees to jelly. It had no effect on me. The burning heat inside of me had turned stone cold. As he pulled off his weapon and began to charge, I stood my ground. Gripping the cool steel of the scythe I felt it become an extension of my body. I swung it in an arc the way Ayres had when he engaged his opponents.

"Come for me," I cried.

And come he did, full tilt with deadly intent etched in every movement he made. Funny how time stands still in life defining moments. With precision I could see the terrible look on his face, fearing all was lost. I noticed his weapon. Saw how it was made to come apart into two pieces—one end given over to his cohort to exact her treachery. Both pieces are meant to go together—perfectly fitted—the way Ayres and I would never be again. What it was about the weapon that so enraged me, I wasn't sure. A combination of things, I suppose: it being the mate of the instrument that had taken Ayres and my friend from me in one fatal moment, and one that would take my life as well. Just as Oro reached me, I closed my eyes. In seconds, I expected my head to be rendered from my body. Not exactly the way I'd ever pictured my death. True, I was angry enough to engage him in battle. But it would only delay the inevitable.

I'll be with you soon, my love.

A hush passed over the land, as though everything and everyone had disappeared. Was I dead, I wondered? Is this how death felt—painless and quiet? I slightly opened one eye, warily thinking perhaps I'd misjudged my foe's proximity.

My other eye sprung open when I saw I no longer stood upon a field of smooth grass. Instead, there were trees all around me. How had that happened? For one terrible second, I thought perhaps Oro had indeed struck off my head and it'd flown far into the forest and I was seeing through dying eyes. But no. My hands still held the scythe; I could feel it in my grip.

But as I looked down, I saw it was no deadly weapon I held.

It was a long, smooth branch.

Further down my eyes traveled, and I realized my feet were not clad in boots. Nor did I wear the black pants of the space uniform. My feet sported runners and I had on a pair of jeans and a long sleeve shirt. I didn't recognize the clothes, didn't know where they came from. Stolen perhaps? Slowly I turned, taking in my surroundings.

I knew this place.

The forest I'd hiked a million times with Uncle Mick surrounded me now. No longer was I on

Taleon. Indeed, had I ever been? Or had it all been an Episode? But I was so sure it'd been real. I released the stick and put a hand to my head—at least it was still attached to my body. So, maybe this was a good thing? Hope suddenly sprang into my chest. If it'd all been an Episode, Ayres may still be alive. And Jack and Danny wouldn't be prisoners on board Baynar's ship. I must have flipped over the edge, as I'd feared in the beginning. There was no other logical explanation. Then again, when had anything in my life ever been logical?

"Now what should I do?" My voice sounded strange echoing through the silent woods. I had to return to the cottage. The last place on Earth I wanted to be, but what choice did I have? It was there or Lindove, and I wasn't ready to face the loony bin yet. What would happen if I went back and discovered Jack and Danny were missing? Maybe they had found me like I remembered, and all of us did go into the cottage. Maybe there hadn't been a tremor, and strange light sucking Danny into the bedroom. What if I'd been the one who'd made them disappear? Who knew what I was capable of anymore?

Or perhaps they were fine? I could've been wandering these woods for minutes, days, or even weeks. Conceivably, this time I may have eluded my keepers for so long that they'd given up on me. I'd have to take the chance the cottage wasn't being monitored. I began to move. Judging by the sky, it'd be dark soon enough. It would only take about ten minutes to get back. At least this time I was unescorted. What my plan would be once I got there, God only knew. What other life did I know but that of Lindove? How could I think to make it in the real world on my own?

And what about Ayres?

Since I'd killed him off in my realistic Episode, maybe he was gone for good? Maybe I'd needed to go through something like that—so life altering—to finally end the insanity?

Would I be free, then?

No more nightmares? No more stalking? No more good boyfriend gone bad? And most especially—no more alien encounters?

The cottage rose up in my line of vision through a haze. Fog had crept across the land, making all appear sinister. Passing through the scorch-marked doors, I entered within. Nothing appeared to have changed.

"Hello?" If the attendants from Lindove were lurking about, I may as well get it over with.

Nothing.

I walked through, opening every door and every window covering, letting in what remained of the light.

My belly growled, and I wondered when the last time I'd eaten was. The cupboards held items that would keep. I boiled the kettle and made a cup of black coffee. Though tired, no way was I ready to sleep. Despite my resolve, as the hours crept on, I finally gave in and lay on the bed in my old room. The pillow and blanket I'd tossed on smelled musty. My last thought before I fell asleep was of Ayres.

What an adventure we'd shared…even if it was all in my head.

Next morning, I awoke and climbed out of bed. I'd slept in my clothes—even the runners—so there was no need to dress. The only change to my wardrobe I made was to swap the shoes for my old hiking boots, which miraculously still fit. As a precaution, I slipped a knife down the inside of my boot—just in case. If I suddenly had to make a dash for it, I wanted to be prepared. I opened a tin of soup and heated it up for breakfast. Eating mechanically, I wondered about my next move.

The television was welcome company. No news about me being a killer at large, at least. Leaning back, I put my feet up and waited. For the first time in as long as I could remember, I had nothing to do. Was this what sanity felt like? Slightly boring perhaps. I closed my eyes and relaxed.

That's when I felt the shaking.

I squeezed my eyes tight, refusing to acknowledge it. But as it grew more violent, I couldn't ignore it any longer. I sat up and watched the windows. Though only mid-morning, all was suddenly dim. The television played static.

"Oh, shit." What would it be this time? Little green men, or perhaps the Grays? Could I dare to hope it may be Ayres?

Blinding light came through the windows. I pulled up my legs and wrapped my arms around them, closing my eyes tight. Once the shaking stopped, I slowly opened my eyes again. There stood a huge man before the window, shrouded in mist or smoke.

"Ayres?" The man took a step toward me, becoming clearer. My eyes widened in alarm. He was not Ayres.

"Kenix, actually," he said.

Kenix? "Ayres' brother? He told me about you."

"I'm flattered." He flashed a chilly smile, reminding me of Ayres.

"You're supposed to be incarcerated."

"Am I?"

"Um, yeah. It's why we went through all the bullshit on Taleon. It's why your brother is...dead." My voice hitched. I couldn't bear it. So it was real then?

"That's where you're wrong," Kenix said, his eyes glinting dangerously. "He's still on Taleon. I'm going there to get him."

I shook my head, trying to clear the fog. "He's alive?"

"I hope so. Or there'll be hell to pay," he said.

"Then what are you waiting for? Go and get him!"

"I need you. Actually, I need the tracker in your head. Taleon's a big place."

"So, take it then," I snapped. God, would it hurt?

"If I remove it, you'll die. You and Ayres are linked. He has the other half in his head. I know he turned it off, but I can turn it back on—through you. Then I can track him with it."

"You're going to kill me then?"

"Unless you come with me," he said.

"I still don't understand how you got away." Besides stalling for time, I really did want to know.

"Plan B," he said, and reached out his hand.

CHAPTER 19

Kenix's ship was about the size of a bus. Not even close to the size of Baynar's. We were both strapped into bucket seats at the front, looking out upon the stars. Once I'd given him my hand, we'd disappeared, only to reappear on board the little craft. He'd hurried to buckle us both in, and then we zoomed away. Earth went from being a huge blue ball to a tiny speck in the distant sky.

I didn't know what was real anymore. But if we were on our way to Ayres, I didn't care. Kenix gripped the control arm of the ship, steering like a pro. We danced around asteroids and whizzing comets that flew through space like projectiles bent on battering us.

"Are you going to tell me what's going on?" I finally asked. He showed no inkling of my concerns.

Instead of answering me, he dug into the pocket of his jacket and pulled out a small mechanism. He turned it on, and it blinked. Then he aimed what appeared to be a laser pointer directly into my eye.

Though it burned, I could not turn away. It caught and held me, making me cry out in fear. "What the hell?" Moments later, it was over. Kenix switched it off and returned it to his pocket.

"It's on now."

Asshole. I assumed he meant my tracker. "How long till we're there?" I shut my eyes and waited for the burning sensation to pass. I didn't feel any different from when the tracker was off. I wasn't sure how the thing worked, but I hoped to hell Kenix would be able to find Ayres with it.

"Not long. Oro was declared champion and taken back on board with his female. The mother ship has returned to Calixtus, so we don't have to worry about avoiding it."

"And how long till they figure out you've escaped?"

"Already have. I'm a wanted man."

Fantastic.

"So what is Plan B? Ayres didn't elaborate."

"With good reason. You had to be believable in order for it to work," Kenix said. "Once Ayres knew the game was rigged, he sent me a signal."

"He did? How?"

"The tournament is viewed by everyone, even on Drone. We had a code word between us. If everything went to shit—and it did—he would say it."

"Into the viewer bubble?"

He looked confused for a moment, then nodded. "I had an escape plan already in place when Ayres told me how he intended to play for my release. Invoking my plan would have me on the run forever. He thought his way was better. And it would have been, except…"

"Except the game was rigged," I said.

"Yeah. I suspected as much. Many of us did."

I digested this information for a bit. "So him getting hurt was part of the plan?"

"Yes. But it wasn't supposed to go down the way it did. That little bitch could have ruined the whole thing."

"So Ayres wanted all of Calixtus to see he was out of the game. Then they'd focus on Oro and the little bitch."

"They were the favorites to win. Baynar had high stakes in this game."

"So how did I end up back on Earth? Why not leave me to rot on Taleon?" I asked.

"Throughout the eundin—year—those viewer bubbles allow us to tune in to see how the losers fare. Baynar couldn't take the chance you'd say anything incriminating."

"So he beamed me home?"

"Up to the ship first. Then put you on a craft like this one, taking you closer to Earth. Then he beamed you home. You would have been out of it the entire time."

"Why not just arrange a little accident for me on Taleon?"

Kenix actually laughed. "And kill off the little tigress? Are you kidding me? They loved you on Calixtus. The way you grabbed Ayres' weapon and went after Oro. You're a bloody hero to them."

Really? So I had done it after all. But I was still confused. "If they loved me, then why did Baynar send me home?"

We both dipped to our left as Kenix skirted around a huge boulder. "They took a poll on what to do with you. The majority of Calixtus wanted you to be allowed to play again. So, just as Oro was about to decapitate you, Baynar intervened. He must have sensed a ratings jump. He froze Oro, you, and the bitch. Then he polled the viewers. Hence, you're alive. To tell you the truth, it was the most exciting thing we'd ever seen a pathetic Earth girl do."

"Gee, thanks." Then another thought struck me. "What about the guys who came on board with me? Jack and Danny?"

"I dunno. If Baynar wanted everything all squared away with you on Earth, he probably returned them as well. It wouldn't have been long before you were put back in the nut house."

"But, how can I play again? I'm not a…virgin."

"Keeping you in the nut house under strict monitoring would ensure you didn't fool around. You wouldn't be a virgin, but there wasn't any fear of you getting pregnant."

"So, he'd just keep me on ice till they found another warrior for me to play the game with next year?" I asked.

"Yeah, and you can imagine the betting war over you. Baynar would stand to gain another fortune in raffling you off."

Holy crap! "I don't know about you, but I would love to blow the lid off that prick's double-dealing."

"What you do with your life after we get Ayres is your business. I, for one, have a price on my head. I intend to move to the other side of the galaxy."

Ayres had said Kenix was all about saving his own ass.

"How do you know they won't be waiting for you on Taleon?" I asked.

"I don't. Ayres risked a lot for me. I can't leave him there to rot." At least he had some sense of loyalty.

Hours later, I estimated, we finally breached the atmosphere of Taleon. We kept low, hoping to stay off any radar that might be monitoring the surface.

Kenix guided the ship to the outer edge of the snowy mountains, and with my guidance, landed in a clearing in the forest, near where I'd last seen Ayres alive. When we hurried to the location, all we saw was blood on the forest floor.

"He's gone," I cried in despair.

"We'll find him. He couldn't have gone far."

We began to walk. Kenix held the laser device in his hand, and every so often, he'd wave it by my head. He seemed to be able to monitor what direction to go by reading the slow or rapid light patterns that blinked on and off on the mechanism.

Even if he hadn't been able to follow the tracker, we probably could have followed Ayres by the trail he'd left on the forest floor. It appeared he'd dragged himself for quite some time. Then the tracks became two solid footprints in the soft mud.

"It looks like he got up," I said, hope encompassing me.

"Or someone carried him," Kenix said.

The trail zigzagged all over the place, coming out by the green field, then going back again into the forest. Night was falling, and I grew antsy. "Shit. Where the hell is he?" Just then, ahead in the distance, we spotted a smooth rock incline. There appeared to be a cave carved into the face.

"There," Kenix said. We rushed over, and Kenix shone a hand light into the interior. Both of us saw the form lying prone on the dirt floor.

"Ayres!" I barreled forward and knelt at his side. Kenix was right behind me, soon kneeling down as well. Before we knew what was happening, a barred gate slammed down over the opening of the cave, trapping us inside.

CHAPTER 20

A blinding flash of light lit up the cave. Seconds later, all three of us were beamed aboard an awaiting ship circling planet Taleon. Baynar, reclined in a chair, his hands steepled beneath his chin, grinned at us like a Cheshire cat.

"Well, look what we have here," he drawled.

Kenix leaped to his feet. "What the hell is this?"

Baynar spread out his hands. "Why, my personal ship, of course. You couldn't expect me to bring you aboard the Lariton?" I guess he meant his bigger ship. "I knew you would return. In fact, I counted on it." He looked at me. "It's unfortunate you were dragged back into this after all the trouble I went to having you set into place on Earth. I hadn't planned on Kenix going after you." He shook his head. "Well, no matter. What's done is done. It won't change anything."

"Why are we here?" Kenix demanded.

"Because I have need of you. Both of you," he nodded at Kenix and I.

All my attention was riveted on Ayres. He breathed, albeit just barely. "I don't know what you want, but whatever it is, I'll do it if you'll help him."

"There's a smart girl," Baynar cheered.

"Give it up. It's only a matter of time before Calixtus figures out what a lying bastard you are," Kenix snapped.

"Temper, temper." Baynar waved his finger. "That kind of attitude won't see me extending any generosity at all."

"Please!" I cried. "Kenix, shut up." My eyes fastened imploringly on Baynar. "Can you help him?"

"For you, certainly," he said. He reached across to a small steel table and pushed a button. Two men hustled in and loaded Ayres onto a stretcher, then whisked him from the room. I stood up and wrung my hands helplessly. If I had to deal with the devil himself to help Ayres, I wouldn't hesitate.

"So where do I figure into this plan of yours?" Kenix asked. "I assume I must be important, otherwise I'd be dead by now."

"Very astute," Baynar said. He gestured to a couple of chairs across from him. Warily, we sat down.

Baynar grilled me with a stare. "As I'm sure he's already told you, you've become quite a favorite on Calixtus. I have to admit, seeing you in action was the most exciting thing..."

I held up a hand. "I know, for such a pathetic

Earth female."

He laughed.

"Kenix told me you wanted me to play again next year. That you planned to raffle me off to the highest bidder," I said.

"Yes, and no. The rules of the tournament say nothing about an Earth female playing the game twice. It's never happened before. They do say, however, that once a warrior begins the game, he cannot compete more than once—whether he's won or not. Once I reveal that Ayres is alive, the population will cry out for you to be allowed to enter with him. Pity that it cannot be allowed. The ratings would've been astronomical."

"So you do plan to raffle me off?"

"On the contrary. Kenix here provides a fantastic alternative. Though he's not Ayres, he's the next best thing. And this time, the roles will be reversed. Kenix will be playing for Ayres' life."

"You're a sick son of a bitch," Kenix growled.

Baynar continued despite the outburst. "Ayres will take your place on Drone—keeping him safe and sound, and assuring you will not flee the galaxy," he said to Kenix.

"And what made you think I would have just gone along with this?" If Ayres' life didn't hang in the balance, I never would have agreed, no matter what they did to me.

Baynar smirked. "Before the game began, I would have told you Ayres was alive, and he was counting on your compliance. It was plain for everyone to see how much you love Ayres. You'll do it for him." He directed his stare to Kenix. "You both will." Then he rubbed his hands together in glee. "Calixtus will be watching you two very carefully. Ayres' faithful brother and his loving Earth girl thrown together in unimaginable circumstances. I wonder what will happen between you two?" He leered at me suggestively.

"You really are a sick son of a bitch," I said. He would have let me mourn Ayres for an entire year if Kenix hadn't come for me. Not to mention leaving me to question my sanity all that time.

"Right now, my personal physician is working to mend your precious Ayres. I'm sure he'll soon be well enough to face Drone. In the meantime, I'll allow you to bid him farewell. Then, after Ayres is deposited safely, I'll see you back to Earth."

"And what do you plan to do with me?" Kenix asked.

"You will return to Calixtus, where I can keep an eye on you. I can't have you rallying your rabble-rousers and breaking Ayres out of Drone. How the devil did you manage to escape?"

Kenix's smile was chilling. "We all have our little secrets."

Baynar rose. "If you'll come with me, you can say your goodbyes."

We got to our feet and followed Baynar out the door. He led us down a few short passageways and then through a door into what appeared to be the physician's room. Ayres lay on a steel bed covered by a blanket. I rushed to his side and gently took his hand. Kenix came over and stood at the other side of the table.

"Ayres? Can you hear me?" He looked so pale. I still feared he was gone.

"He's asleep," a man said, coming up to stand near me.

"Will he be all right?" I asked, assuming he was the physician.

He was kindly looking, and he actually smiled at me. "He'll be fine."

Kenix and I breathed a sigh of relief.

Ayres' eyes suddenly began to flutter, and his grip on my hand tightened. He coughed and then opened his eyes. "Amanda?"

I beamed at him. "Yes. It's me. And look, Kenix is here too."

Ayres peered at his brother and smiled. "You're

free." Then his eyes focused on Baynar, who'd moved closer to the table. "Dammit."

"I'm glad to see you recovered, Ayres. Calixtus will rejoice," Baynar said.

"You can't send him to Drone. He's too weak. They'll eat him alive," Kenix said.

Ayres stared at his brother, confused. "Drone? What do you mean?"

Baynar came closer to the table. "He'll be kept in isolation until he's stronger. Besides, no one would want to damage the prize of the next tournament."

Ayres tried to rise, but the physician gently pushed him back down. "Take it easy," he told him. "You'll only hurt your recovery."

"What the hell is going on?" Ayres demanded.

Baynar quickly filled Ayres in on his plans for all of us—leaving out the part of my little heroics. All the while, Ayres' face grew grimmer. "Bastard," he said.

"Say your goodbyes," Baynar snapped. "You have five eudn." He turned and left the room.

I took it to mean we had five minutes. Not much time.

"What happened on Taleon after I fell?" Ayres asked me.

I felt as if this was all my fault. If I hadn't been

so enraged and taken off after Oro and Lissa, this wouldn't be happening. "I took your scythe and went after them," I admitted.

"You what?" demanded Ayres. "I told you to protect yourself with it. Not to seek revenge."

"I was so mad. Oro was fine—everything Lissa said was a lie. I saw them strolling across the field toward the Safe Zone, and I couldn't let them get away with it."

Ayres closed his eyes. "What did you do?"

"I knocked her down and waited for Oro to come at me. I didn't kill her."

"Before Oro could get to her, Baynar intervened," Kenix said. "He sent her back to Earth, and then hatched this little plan to have us play for your life. Calixtus went wild over Amanda. Baynar expects the ratings to skyrocket next year."

"So I'm to go to Drone, and Amanda will return to Earth. And you?" Ayres asked.

"Baynar wants me on Calixtus, where he can keep watch on me. He's worried I'll try to break you out of Drone."

"Even if you did, he'd just use Amanda's implant to track me down."

Damn the stupid piece of technology in my brain.

"He'll be putting one in me next, I suppose," Kenix said.

"You guys didn't have a Plan C, by chance?" I asked hopefully.

"No. Plan B was to have me break out of Drone—no easy task—and then come for Ayres on Taleon. Everyone would think him dead anyway, so they wouldn't ask any questions."

What about me? How did I figure into their plan?

Ayres squeezed my hand. "You would have come with us," he said, reading my mind. "You are mine."

I gulped. His determined stare pierced right through me.

Mine?

Was that a good thing, or a bad thing?

CHAPTER 21

Our five minutes were up. It was time to say goodbye. Despite Kenix and the physician's presence, I bent and gave Ayres a lingering kiss on the lips. I couldn't believe we'd be forced to spend a year apart. And then I'd be forced to play that hellish game again, without him by my side. At least I knew he was alive.

"I'm so glad you're all right," I said. "I'm sorry."

"Sorry for what?"

I couldn't stand the guilt. "If it weren't for me, you guys would be free."

"No. If it weren't for you, I'd probably be dead," Ayres said.

"It's true. Without your tracker, I may not have found him till it was too late," Kenix said. I knew he was being kind. He probably hadn't needed my help at all. I had the feeling he'd brought me along to save him and Ayres a trip later. With this thing in my head, the authority on Calixtus would no doubt have used me to track them both, figuring they'd be together. Kenix needed to make sure I was no threat to them—one way or another.

"I shouldn't have let my guard down," Ayres said.

"Don't worry. I got her for you." Even though she was probably living it up right now, with Oro.

"Keep your head down on Drone. Don't make any enemies, and watch your back," Kenix told him. They grasped forearms in a warrior's farewell.

"Don't worry," the physician said. "He'll make a full recovery." He seemed a nice enough guy. I wondered how he'd wound up working for Baynar.

"Please be careful," I said.

"I will," Ayres promised. "You too." He looked at his brother. "And you."

Kenix nodded. Slowly, we headed for the door. When we got out into the hallway, the door swished shut, cutting off my eye contact with Ayres. There were two guys waiting to escort us back to Baynar.

We got halfway down the hallway before all hell broke loose. An alarm went off, distracting the guards. Kenix reacted quickly, punching one man in the face, knocking him senseless to the ground. When the other guard advanced on him, Kenix spun around and kicked him in the side of the head. I stood there staring at the two unconscious men.

"What the hell are you doing?" Baynar would kill us both for this.

Kenix shrugged and grinned roguishly. "Plan C?"

A few seconds later, Ayres joined us in the hall. I rushed over to him, noticing he was half-dressed. He had on pants and boots and was pulling on a shirt over his bandage. "What are you doing up? You're hurt."

"I'm well enough," he said. I knew that look on his face all too well—he was in warrior mode.

"Physician?" Kenix handed Ayres one of the guards' weapons and had taken one for himself. They looked like mini ray guns.

Ayres nodded. "Not before he hit the alarm, though."

"You didn't kill him, did you?" I asked.

"No," Ayres said. "How many on board?"

"Six, I believe. Judging by the size of the vessel," Kenix said. "Three are handled." He looked down at the guards. He fiddled with his weapon and shot a laser bolt into each of them. "They won't wake up till it's all over."

"And here I was hoping for a challenge," said Ayres.

"So where are you going now?" I asked.

"To find Baynar," Kenix said.

The ship was small, so it didn't take us long to retrace our steps to where Baynar had first teleported us. The alarm still sounded, so he obviously knew something was up. When we reached the last corner, Kenix went around first. He jumped back in a hurry as a riot of laser shots swirled out—those ones set to kill, judging by the scorch marks they left. All of us flattened against the wall.

"You stay here." Ayres gave me that look when I frowned at him. "Ready?" he said to Kenix.

"As I'll ever be."

Both of them started around the corner, ray guns blazing. After a firestorm of blasting lights and curse words, finally, all was silent. "You can come out now," Ayres called. Just as I was about to join them, I felt a poke in my back.

"Don't move," Baynar's voice came from behind me.

When I failed to appear or say anything, both brothers came looking for me. They stopped dead when they saw Baynar standing behind me.

"Let her go," Ayres said. The look in his eyes scared even me.

"You can't win," Kenix told him. "There's no one left on board alive to help you," he lied.

"You can't handle the ship and keep an eye on all of us," Ayres said. "The moment you turn your back, you're a dead man."

"Not if I kill you both now," Baynar said.

"No!" I cried.

"That'll be bad for ratings," Kenix told him.

"You wouldn't want to kill your star attractions," Ayres taunted.

"You're right. I can stun you, though." I felt Baynar's weapon shift around slightly. While he concentrated his attention on keeping watch on the brothers and fiddling with the settings on his gun, I reached down. Slowly, I lifted my foot and withdrew the long, thin blade from my boot. Holding the hilt in my hand, I quickly flipped the blade upward so it rested hidden against the inside of my wrist. I locked eyes with Ayres. He'd seen what I had done. Instead of aggravation, I saw the look of hope on his face. His lips even curled into a smile.

"What're you smiling about, idiot?" Baynar demanded. "Are you thinking about Drone? Why don't you tell him how delightful it is, Kenix? I'm sure you enjoyed your stay immensely."

"Actually, I'm wondering how you'll enjoy spending your last days playing for survival on Taleon?" Ayres said. "That's where I plan to send you when we take your ship and leave you to rot."

Baynar laughed. "What a fool you are. As you can see, I'm the one making the decisions here.

You'll be the one to rot until your brother wins your freedom—if he doesn't manage to screw it up." His other hand came up to fondle my hair. "I wonder what will happen to your little Amanda, spending days and nights alone with your brother? Relying on him for… everything?"

Ayres, angry now, took a step forward. Baynar shifted the gun in my back. "That's far enough!" When Ayres took another step, I struck. Raising my arm, I angled the blade. With all the strength I could muster, I stabbed it into Baynar's thigh.

He screamed in agony.

Ayres leapt forward and grabbed the hand I stretched out to him. He threw me into Kenix, who shoved me behind his back. Peeking around his bulk, I saw Baynar grapple for his weapon. He was on his knees now and lifted his head just as Ayres punched him in the face. Baynar dropped like a stone.

"Shit!" Kenix said. "That went well."

Ayres stared at me for a moment, perhaps making sure I was unharmed. Satisfied, he turned his attention to his foe. He grabbed Baynar and tossed him over his shoulder. "Let's get him and the others to the transporter."

"So you really mean to leave him on Taleon?" Kenix asked.

"Yes. Something tells me the bloodthirsty crowd on Calixtus won't intervene."

"Too bad we can't stick around and watch that," Kenix said.

We entered the room with the transporter, and Ayres laid Baynar down. He then led me to a chair and made me sit. Once seated, I realized I was shaking.

"We're going to get the others," Ayres told me.

"There may still be a few roaming around," Kenix reminded him. Ayres shrugged.

"They'll all be meeting the same fate soon enough," Ayres predicted. "We won't be long, all right?"

I nodded.

Not much later, six men were piled together on the floor of the transporter and beamed down to Taleon's surface.

"Won't they be in for a shock when they wake up?" Kenix said with a chuckle.

Ayres kneeled down before me and took my hand. "Are you sure you're all right, Amanda?"

"I think so."

"Kenix and I are going somewhere safe across the galaxy. We're both hunted men now. We can't return to Calixtus."

Kenix shrugged. "I knew once I escaped Drone,

I'd be on the run. It beats the alternative." He gave me a wink and left the room.

"I'm sorry," I said.

"Don't be. I will not miss Calixtus. We were wrong to use your world, your people, just as we're wrong to use Taleon and the Varlings. We have no right."

"What changed your mind?" I asked.

"You did. Getting to know you, to…love you."

"What?" Did I hear him right? I got the feeling those words were as alien to him as I was.

He leaned forward and kissed me. "I said I love you. I meant to tell you before I passed out. Now, what I'm wondering is whether you wish to return to Earth? I can't guarantee you'll be safe there from my kind."

I was still trying to wrap my head around the idea that he loved me. "You're afraid they'll use the device in my head to track you down."

"They may try. They may also want to use you in the next tournament. I hear you're quite popular."

I noticed the gleam in his eye. "But, Baynar's gone. Everyone thinks you're dead," I reminded him.

"If Baynar isn't rescued from Taleon, there will always be another asshole to take his place. You can bet he'll tell the world what happened here—at least, his version of it. It's just a matter of time before Calixtus knows I'm alive."

He could never return home anyway, since he was supposed to be rotting on Taleon like the rest of the contestants that lost the game—the ones who survived. "So you'll spend your life on the run?"

"Like Kenix said, it's better than the alternative. The choice is yours, Amanda. I know Earth is your home."

Was it? I'd been controlled and manipulated since I was a child. How long would it take for someone to hunt me down and use me again? Not that I'd be hard to find, locked up helpless in the loony bin. Even if Ayres dropped me somewhere else, what would I do? I had no skills. What I did have was a device in my head that might possibly make me unsafe anywhere on the surface of Earth. Would I be safe anywhere in the galaxy? Would Ayres?

He seemed to read my mind. "Where we're going, it'll be impossible to track us...especially if we're together," he added.

"You don't leave me much choice," I said.

"You always have a choice." Seeing the determination on his face, I didn't quite believe him. After all, he'd said 'you're mine'.

"What do you want me to do?" Part of me still feared he didn't want me by his side.

He smiled. "I want you with me. Always."

I smiled back. So, what was it to be? Life on the run on Earth, or a life of adventure zooming around the universe? Who knew what was destined for me next? This time, however, I would be the one deciding my fate. No longer would I be a pawn in anyone's game. The thought was frightening. Terrifying actually. But look at what I'd already faced and still come out alive. Plus, I wasn't alone anymore. At my side would be the man I'd grown to love. Together we could do anything.

"I'll go with you."

"You won't regret it, Amanda. I'll keep you safe," he vowed.

And as he hugged me tight, I somehow knew he'd keep his word.

Juliet is an award-winning author of several best-selling novels and short stories. She lives in Ontario with her husband, cat, and dog. You can check out Juliet's website to see what she's been up to.
http://JulietCardinWebsite.Yolasite.com

www.ingramcontent.com/pod-product-compliance
Lightning Source LLC
LaVergne TN
LVHW090607110826
845146LV00001B/294

* 9 7 9 8 8 9 1 2 6 5 3 6 3 *